P9-DMG-292

DONAVAN'S DOUBLE TROUBLE

MONALISA DEGROSS

DONAVAN'S DOUBLE TROUBLE

ILLUSTRATED BY
AMY BATES

Amistad
AN IMPRINT OF HARPERCOLLINS*PUBLISHERS*

Amistad is an imprint of HarperCollins Publishers.

Donavan's Double Trouble

www.harpercollinschildrens.com

Library of Congress Cataloging-in-Publication Data
DeGross, Monalisa.

Donavan's double trouble / Monalisa DeGross ; illustrated by Amy Bates. —
1st ed.

p. cm.

Summary: Fourth-grader Donavan is sensitive about the problems he has understanding math, and then when his favorite uncle, a former high school basketball star, returns from National Guard duty an amputee, Donavan's problems get even worse as he struggles to accept this "new" Uncle Vic.

ISBN 978-0-06-077293-2 (trade bdg.)

ISBN 978-0-06-077294-9 (lib. bdg.)

[1. Amputees—Fiction. 2. People with disabilities—Fiction. 3. Uncles—Fiction. 4. Math anxiety—Fiction. 5. Schools—Fiction. 6. African Americans—Fiction.] I. Bates, Amy June, ill. II. Title.

PZ7.D3643Dd 2007 2007011244
[Fic]—dc22 CIP
AC

Typography by Christopher Stengel
1 2 3 4 5 6 7 8 9 10

First Edition

To Henry G. Coleman and Vic Carter DeGross:
we remember

CONTENTS

DONAVAN'S DOUBLE TROUBLE

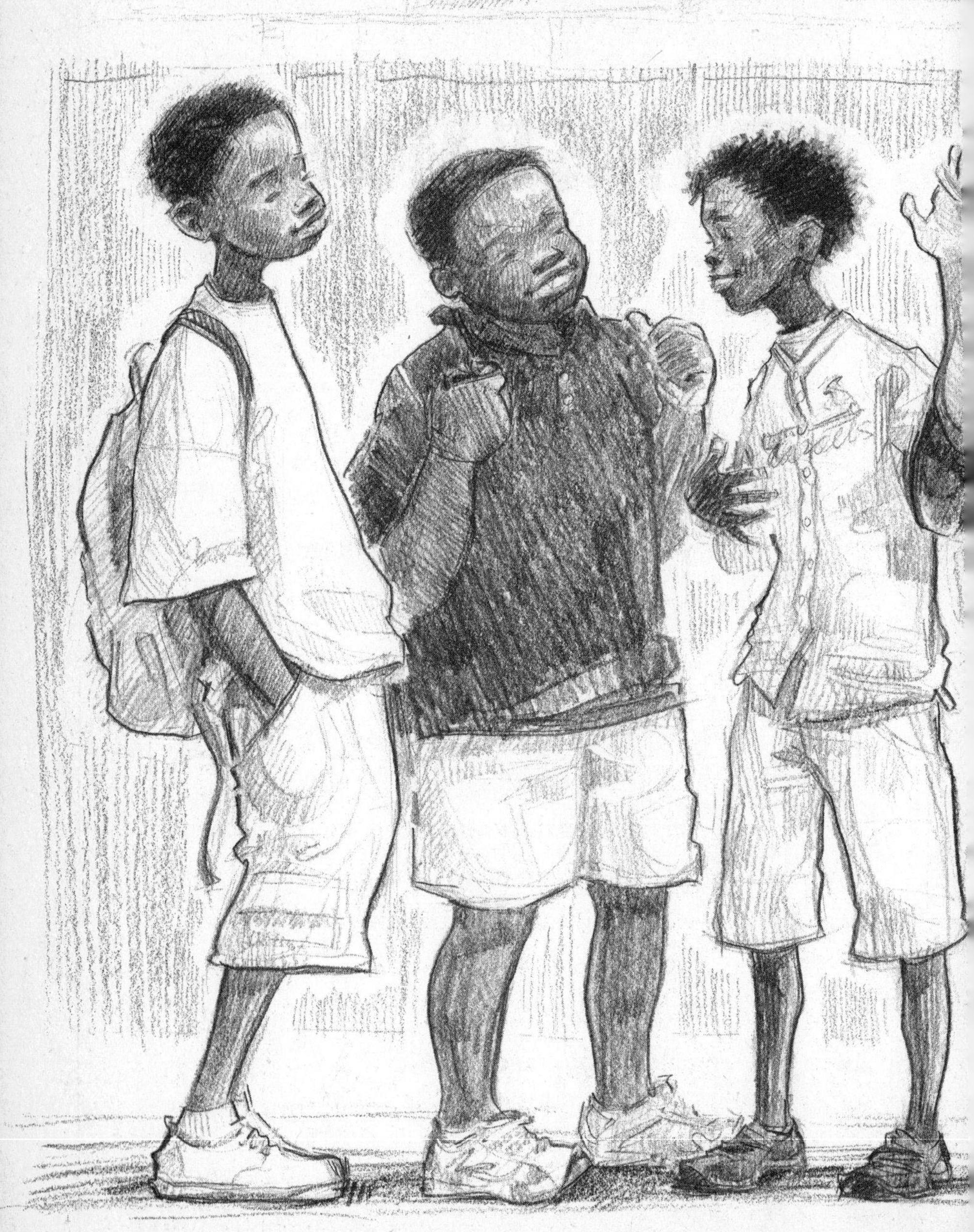
HERITA

MONTH

CHAPTER 1

HERITAGE MONTH

"Donavan, who are you bringing to Heritage Month?" Pooh asked, his words muffled by the chunk of apple in his mouth.

The bell rang. Lunch was over for fourth and fifth graders. Donavan slung his backpack over his shoulder and picked up his lunch tray.

"No one," he answered, heading for the large green trash can near the exit. Pooh tossed his apple core on the tray and followed Donavan into the noisy hall.

"No one?" Pooh asked, his eyes wide.

"No one," Donavan repeated, walking faster. "I haven't been thinking about Heritage Month."

"Huh? After Valentine's Day nobody thinks about

anything else," Pooh said, hurrying to keep up. "Hey, wait."

Donavan could tell by the sound of Pooh's voice that his friend did not believe him. "I got other things I'm thinking about," he said, and looked at Pooh as if he were a pesky fly.

"What things?"

"Math things: problems, quizzes, tests, homework."

"Oh!" Pooh knew that math was Donavan's worst subject. "Well, I got some good, big news. It's gonna cheer you up." Pooh waited a few seconds.

"Oh yeah?" Donavan kept walking.

"Pop Grandville is coming to Heritage Month!" Pooh paused. "He's gonna bring his new film." Pause. "It's about kids in a South African township."

Donavan stopped suddenly. Pooh bumped against his backpack, but he never stopped talking.

"They're our age and the film shows them hanging out and doing their thing."

Donavan really hadn't been thinking about Heritage Month. But he had to admit it, this film might be good. Better than good. Kids from Africa! "We'll get to hear their music. See the type of video games they play?"

Pooh joined in. "Sports, food, clothes. Man, we get to see how they hang out South African style."

"Yeah, but this is what I want to see. How they dance!"

Donavan stomped his feet and clapped his hands. He danced around in a circle to his own beat.

Several kids stopped and watched. "What ya doing, D?" someone asked.

Before Donavan could explain, Pooh waved his hand in a warning. Donavan looked up and saw Miss Strickland, the hall monitor, staring in his direction.

"Nothing," he mumbled, and started walking again. The last thing he wanted was Miss Strickland's attention. She loved handing out detention slips.

Pooh followed. "Hey, let's keep this quiet," he whispered. "I want Pop to be a big surprise. I mean B-I-G big."

Donavan nodded. "Okay. I just got excited. Your grandpop is so cool. His pictures are in magazines big-time."

"Oh yeah. Do you still have the autographed copy of *National Geographic*?"

"Sure do. It was my first autograph." Donavan shook his head. "I can't believe I know someone who makes movies. How come he's not off somewhere filming something?" Pooh was always telling Donavan how he wished his grandfather were around more.

"He is, but when we visited him last summer I told him about Heritage Month. I told him that any family member could come, but that we wanted seniors."

"Yeah, everybody wants to hear about how things were in the old days," Donavan agreed.

"My mom and dad explained how Ms. Cassel started Heritage Month so that grandparents and parents could talk to us about family history," Pooh continued.

Donavan imitated Ms. Cassel's voice: "Youngsters, you must learrrrrrrn about your culllllllture."

"Donnie, you should have heard Pop laugh when I told him about Mr. Reynolds and his bagpipes."

"Did you tell him how his kilt fell down?" Donavan gave Pooh a high five.

"Yup. And I also showed Pop how Mr. Ang acted out each of the animals in the Chinese horoscope."

"The tiger, brave and dangerous." Donavan struck a pose and raised his fist.

"The dog, loyal and courageous." Pooh bumped his fist against Donavan's.

"Pooh, you should have told him about Ms. Martinez's piñata and how we couldn't break it no matter how hard we tried," Donavan said.

"I forgot about that. But I did tell him that the whole school celebrates for a month," Pooh said. "I told him about the food, the costumes people wear, and a whole bunch of other stuff. He was really into it." Donavan could tell by Pooh's voice that his friend was excited. He was laughing and talking at the same time, getting louder and louder with each word.

"Your grandpop is like a celebrity. Everyone's gonna love him." Donavan held his hand up and made a victory sign. "Heritage Month is gonna be awesome this year."

Donavan looked up and saw Eric, his other best buddy, weaving his way through the crowd toward them. The three boys had been friends since kindergarten. Miz Utz, the school's office manager, always called them "triple trouble."

"What's up? Whatsup? Whatsup?" Eric asked, when he caught up with them.

"Hey, where were you at lunch?" Pooh asked.

"Principal's office."

"Huh?" said Donavan.

"No trouble." Eric laughed. "I had to give Ms. Cassel a note from my grandma." Eric looked left and right and then lowered his voice. "Grandma is coming to Heritage Month. She's going to teach batik to the fourth and fifth grades."

Donavan nudged Pooh. They knew that Eric liked everything he did to be mysterious.

"Nice," Pooh said.

"What's batik? Is she weaving something?" Donavan pictured the wooden loom and spinning wheel he'd seen in Eric's grandma's workroom.

"No, batik is a different kind of thing," Eric explained. "She'll use hot wax and dye." The boys listened while Eric explained his grandmother's work in detail, talking as if he were the expert.

"Pop Grandville is coming," Pooh interrupted Eric.

"And bringing a movie about kids in South Africa," Donavan added.

"You're lucky," Eric said wistfully.

Donavan knew Eric was wishing he had someone as cool as Pop Grandville to bring. He did too. Donavan thought for a moment and could think of no one. Eric cupped his hands around his mouth and called, "Earth to Donnie! Earth to Donnie! What you thinking about so hard, homeboy? You got a secret?"

"No. Do you?" Donavan said.

"Maybe," Eric said, and winked his eye. "Who you bringing to Heritage Month?"

"No one," Pooh answered for Donavan.

"No one?" Eric echoed.

"No one," Donavan said, exasperated. "Gimme a break, y'all. It's not like I never had a guest. Remember when my grandfather came and showed us how shoes were made in the old days?"

"True, true," Eric said. "Boy, those shoes looked crazy. I remember a pair that you needed a long, skinny black hook to button."

"Wouldn't it be great if we had a triple hitter?" Pooh asked. "All of us together."

"True, true." Donavan glanced down the hall and noticed Mr. Sullivan, his math teacher, standing outside his classroom. Math! He had enough troubles on his mind without worrying about who to invite for Heritage Month. "I think Ms. Cassel has enough people," he said.

"Nope," Eric said. "I heard her tell Miz Utz that she wished she had a few more guests."

"There's Mr. Sullivan," Donavan said loudly. "We'd better get to class."

"Man oh man, it's lima-bean time." Pooh shook his head.

"Yup," Donavan agreed. Whenever one of them had to face something that they hated, they called it lima-bean time.

"How you doing in his class, Donnie?" Eric asked.

"The same." Donavan's shoulders slumped a little.

Eric shook his finger at Donavan and said in a deep voice, "Buddy-boy, math is like lima beans. It puts a bad taste in your mouth."

Pooh patted Donavan on the shoulder and added, "But it's good for you."

Donavan groaned and followed his friends down the hall.

WASABI
WASABI
WASABI

CHAPTER 2

HAVING A HARD TIME

"That class lasted a hundred years!" Donavan pulled his books from his locker and slammed the door. He looked at Eric and frowned. "No matter how much I study, I just bomb out."

"It stinks," Eric said. "I know you been trying."

"Why does Mr. Sullivan keep calling on you?" Pooh said in disgust. "He *knows* you don't know the answers."

"I know half of the answers," Donavan retorted, pushing past Pooh.

"Pooh," Eric said, "that didn't help." He ran after Donavan.

The boys walked home in silence until Pooh tried again to make Donavan feel better. "Cheer up,

Donnie, it's Friday!"

"Yup, it's Friday, and you know what they say." Eric began to rhyme. "No more quizzes, no more books. No more teachers' dirty looks."

Donavan added a rhyme. "No more pencils, no more chalk. No more teachers' talk, talk, talk."

"Hey, that's cool," Pooh said, pulling his hat down over his ears.

"It's not cool, it's cold." Donavan's teeth had started to chatter. "Spring better hurry up and get here."

Eric snapped his fingers. "I just remembered something that might help you with math."

Donavan looked surprised. He'd thought they were finished discussing school. "What is it?" he asked cautiously.

"I just remembered something I heard on a TV talk show," Eric said, thoughtful. "I didn't hear everything; I was just passing through the living room." He hesitated.

"What was it, Eric?" Donavan asked impatiently.

"Well, I don't know if you've ever heard of a math block." He glanced at Donavan, who looked skeptical. Eric continued. "But from what I heard from that expert on TV, I think that's what you've got."

Pooh looked puzzled. "What in the world is a math block?"

Donavan shook his head. He knew that Eric was

getting ready to talk like he was the expert. *I hope this makes sense,* he thought.

"Welll, let me explain." Eric rubbed his chin. "A math block is when a person just can't understand math. No matter what they do, or how hard they try, they just don't get math."

Donavan continued walking and staring ahead. He already knew that he didn't get math. So far Eric wasn't being much help at all.

"Why?" Pooh asked.

"Because something, something they don't know about is blocking their mind. That something—that they don't know about—keeps them from understanding how math works."

"So what happens to them?" Pooh glanced at Donavan.

"Wellll," Eric said again, scratching his head this time. "They just keep trying things, everything, anything, until they have a math breakthrough." He nodded his head and smiled as if he had just solved the problem.

"What blocks them?" Pooh asked again.

"Pooh, don't ask so many questions," Eric said, scowling.

"But really, what blocks them?" Pooh persisted.

Eric shrugged. "I don't know." His voice got louder.

"I only know that for some reason they can't understand math."

"And?" Pooh continued, and looked over at Donavan.

Eric was so annoyed that his voice boomed. "THEY have to keep trying OLD things, NEW things, ANYTHING, until something clicks and breaks through the block." Eric punched his hands in the air to make his point. "And when that CLICK happens, it's called a breakthrough." Eric ignored Pooh and looked directly at Donavan. "Try everything," he ordered. "Until you break through the block."

"What if there's no click?" Pooh asked, hunching his shoulders. "What happens then?"

"Later, guys," Donavan said, and veered across the street. He knew that Pooh would ask more and more questions until Eric's answers would get as tangled as a bowl of spaghetti. He was through listening to them.

"Hey, where you going?" Pooh called in surprise.

"Home." Donavan didn't turn around.

Pooh and Eric looked at each other.

"Pooh, you're so annoying. Why did you have to ask so many questions?" Eric shook his head.

"I can't help it," Pooh said, shrugging. "I was trying to understand the block and then the break and then you added the click. Sorry."

Eric watched Donavan walk away. "Wellll, maybe

he's thinking about it." Eric grinned. "Come on, buddy."

"Will just thinking about the math block break it?" Pooh asked.

"Maybe," Eric said, but he did not sound like he believed it.

"Man oh man," Donavan mumbled as he walked home. He liked his best buddies, but sometimes he needed to be alone. He didn't want to hear them talk about his math problems and he definitely didn't want to think about his math problems. Eric had one thing right: He really had a math block.

Sometimes, in class, Donavan understood the equations and could follow along step by step. But when he went to the board to do a problem or got home and started his homework, he was lost.

"What am I gonna do?" he whispered. Just thinking about his math problems gave him the blues.

"Hello, young man."

Donavan looked over his shoulder and saw Mr. Ang walking toward him, carrying a stack of cardboard boxes. The boxes were piled so high that Donavan could barely see Mr. Ang's face.

"Hello, Mr. Ang. How ya doing?" He slowed his steps.

"I am doing A-O.K." Mr. Ang grunted, breathing

hard. The boxes looked heavy. Donavan ran ahead and opened the door to the grocery store that the Angs owned.

"Thank you, Donavan." Mr. Ang walked up the steps and through the opened door. Donavan followed him inside.

Sharp and spicy smells teased Donavan's nose. "Something smells good." He inhaled and tried to guess. "Soup?" Sniff. "Cookies?" Sniff, sniff. "Ummm. Where's Mrs. Ang? She must be cooking."

Mr. Ang sniffed the air. "Smells like ginger cakes are baking." The warmth in the store made his round glasses fog. He dropped the boxes on the floor and reached into his coat. "Whew!" Pulling out his handkerchief, he took off his glasses to wipe them. "Donnie, good to see you. Did you know that I'm coming to Heritage Month?"

Donavan's mouth dropped open. Mr. Ang smiled. "Nikki invited me."

His little sister had done that? "But Mr. Ang, you already came to Heritage Month. Remember? You talked about the Chinese horoscope."

"Yes. Yes, I remember that. Ms. Cassel invited me, but this time I am Nikki's guest." Mr. Ang resettled his glasses on his face.

Donavan still wore a surprised expression. "She didn't tell me."

"Hello, word boy." Mrs. Ang emerged from the back

room, carrying her baby daughter. "Still collecting words?"

"Yes. And I still keep them in a jar." Donavan leaned over and looked at the baby, who gurgled and waved her arms. "Howdy, baby Jolie."

"Nikki visited us last Sunday to see baby Jolie," Mr. Ang said. "When Nikki saw my great-grandfather's abacus on the mantel, she asked me a million questions."

"Your counting thing?"

"Yes, my counting thing. I told Nikki the history of the abacus and how my great-grandfather, grandfather, and father all used it in China." Mr. Ang took Jolie from his wife and began making funny faces.

"Did you show her how to use it?" Donavan reached over to tickle Jolie.

"A little bit. Nikki learns very, very fast. She thought her class might like to know about my ancient calculator." Mr. Ang kissed the baby's fingers. "It will be a while before I can come to school for Jolie. I'm so glad Nikki invited me."

"Me too." Of course Nikki would like Mr. Ang's abacus. She loved anything to do with numbers. "Mr. Ang, do you think your abacus could help me?" Donavan asked.

Mr. Ang laughed as though Donavan had told a big joke. "It helped my ancestors, Donavan. I don't know about now."

Donovan patted Jolie on the cheek. He really didn't want to think about math things. "I got to get home. I'll see y'all later."

"See you later." The Angs, even Jolie, waved goodbye.

During the walk home, Donavan remembered what Pooh had said about "a triple hitter." Pooh was right. It would be fun if the three of them could each bring a cool guest to Heritage Month. But who could he ask? He hadn't been thinking about Heritage Month. Getting his math grade up had been the main thing on his mind.

He'd studied and studied for his last quiz and he thought he'd passed it. But when Mr. Sullivan returned the papers, Donavan looked at the grade circled in red and at the red *x*'s all over the page and felt hot with shock and disappointment. It was like a firecracker had exploded in his head. He still remembered folding the paper into a tiny square and stuffing it in his backpack. He never wanted to see it again.

He shook the memory out of his head. *All I do is think about math, math, and math. I am gonna block my math block out,* he thought. *Yeah, that's what I'm gonna do. Think about something good.*

How can I be part of Heritage Month? he wondered.

What can I do? I don't have a guest or an exhibit. Maybe, maybe . . . He slowed his steps. Maybe he could be a greeter! The greeters welcomed guests and showed them around the school. All of the greeters were fifth graders, but he might be able to talk Ms. Cassel into letting him join. Maybe Eric and Pooh would want to be greeters too.

"Oh yeah!" He stopped to do a victory dance. He liked this idea. He'd get to meet all the guests before the other kids. He knew for sure he could talk Pooh and Eric into trying to convince Ms. Cassel. He added an extra step to his dance.

I might even get the chance to explain a big exhibit, he thought. *If I practice enough I'll sound like an expert.* He was beginning to feel good. He pushed his math problems out of his head.

CHAPTER 3

HAPPIER TIMES

Donavan found Nikki at the kitchen table, wrapping a bright orange napkin around a fork, a knife, and a spoon.

"What you doing?" he asked, and plopped down.

"Making sure there's enough silverware for everybody coming to dinner on Sunday." She rolled the napkin into a neat bundle and then tied it with a piece of yellow yarn.

"How many you making?" It didn't look like she was counting, and he knew that Nikki liked to count everything.

"I'm making ten bundles and there are three in each bundle." She continued working. "Where you been?"

Uncle

"I just saw Mr. Ang and he said you invited him to Heritage Month." Donavan picked up a napkin and looked at the tiny flowers printed on it.

Nikki kept making new bundles. "He's my first guest for Heritage Month and he's bringing his abacus. It's an ancient calculator from China. Mr. Ang says the abacus has been in his family for five generations."

"Who told you to invite him to school?" He liked to tease Nikki. He knew she hated it when he doubted her.

"I told myself." She stuck her tongue out. "And then I went to school and told Ms. Cassel about Mr. Ang's abacus. And then I told her I'd invited him to Heritage Month." Nikki started another bundle. "Ms. Cassel said, 'Nikki, that's wooonderful. Thank you for bringing him to Herrrrrritage Month.'" Donavan laughed because Nikki sounded just like Ms. Cassel.

"How come you're not counting the bundles?" He wondered if Nikki was going to forget how many she'd made. There was a big pile of them on the table already.

"I'm counting in my head," she answered. "Want me to tell you how?"

"Nope." Donavan began folding a napkin. He watched to see if Nikki's lips were moving. They weren't.

She was counting silently and talking at the same time.

"We're going to have a lot of fun on Sunday," Nikki said.

"You say that every time the whole family comes to dinner," Donavan grumbled.

"But this Sunday is special," Nikki insisted. "Uncle Vic is coming. We haven't seen him since August and it's already February."

"Oh," Donavan said quietly. With his mind on math and Heritage Month, he'd forgotten about Uncle Vic's welcome-home dinner.

"Grandma says he just got his new legs." Nikki began to stack her bundles in the basket that sat on the table. "I can't wait to see him walk." Her eyes brightened. "Grandma says he won't have to go back in the hospital anymore. Aren't you excited?"

"I just forgot about Sunday dinner," Donavan muttered, and got up from the table to open the refrigerator.

"Donnie," Nikki said. "I've got a great idea. You should make Uncle Vic a word jar." Nikki loved Donavan's word jar. He collected words—from everywhere—wrote them on slips of paper and kept them in a large jar. "You probably have lots of words that say how happy we are that Uncle Vic is coming home for good."

"Why don't you do it?" Donavan snapped, and picked up a jar of jam.

"Because you know the best words." She watched him gather crackers and peanut butter. "Aren't you glad Uncle Vic has new legs? How come you aren't acting happy?"

Donavan put the jam, peanut butter, and crackers on the counter and began to fix a snack. He didn't know how to answer her question, and suddenly he felt angry.

"Anyway, I already made him a friendship bracelet. Donnie?" Nikki asked softly as she placed the last bundle of silverware neatly in the basket. "Why are you acting like a grumpy Gus?"

He did not answer.

"See ya later, Gus," Nikki called, and left the kitchen.

"Sorry, Nikki," Donavan whispered. His stomach felt tight. He had not meant to be grumpy with his sister.

"Dag!" he said to no one as he sat down with his snack. Uncle Vic was coming home and that was a good thing. *It's a great thing,* Donavan thought. *He's got new legs and that's happy news.* So why, he wondered, did he feel like Mr. Sullivan had just announced a pop quiz? A while ago math seemed like his biggest problem. Now it was seeing Uncle Vic again.

Donavan frowned and crunched the salty crackers, sticky with jam and peanut butter. He didn't want to put Uncle Vic in the same category as math, no way. Math thoughts made him feel unsure and unhappy.

Before the war, before his uncle had lost his legs, the thought of Uncle Vic coming to dinner would have made Donavan glad. Now the thought of seeing his favorite uncle in a wheelchair or walking on artificial legs made him feel almost as bad as when his math homework was a mess and he couldn't make it right.

One day long ago, after a basketball game, Uncle Vic had said to him, "You and I make the perfect uncle-and-nephew team." It was so true then. His uncle had been his favorite person.

Uncle Vic had given Donavan his first basketball hoop. It was in the backyard and Donavan still practiced on it. Whenever Uncle Vic would come around, the two of them would shoot basket after basket.

He smiled when he remembered how Uncle Vic ducked and dodged around the backyard, moving as if he were in an NBA game. He dribbled in circles; he spun around and around. Donavan loved watching his uncle's basketball dance. He'd taught Donavan so many smooth moves.

Donavan pushed his snack aside, folded his arms,

and cradled his head on them. It felt good to remember Uncle Vic before he went away to war with his National Guard unit. Before the tank he was riding in got blown up and Uncle Vic lost his legs. He wished Uncle Vic hadn't gone off to war. He wished he'd been riding in some other tank, one that hadn't hit a bomb. Sometimes he even wished somebody else's uncle had been riding in that tank instead.

Donavan's thoughts started racing, so he switched his mind back to the old days. He remembered Uncle Vic on Saturday afternoons, teaching Donavan and Nikki dances with names like the cabbage patch, the snake, and the running man. Nikki and he would try to follow the steps, but it was more fun just to watch Uncle Vic.

All Donavan's memories were of a joking, laughing, dancing, always moving Vic Carter. There was not one single memory where Uncle Vic was standing still. That was how Donavan had always thought of his uncle until the day he'd walked into the kitchen and seen his parents and grandmother sitting at the table with wet faces. The cheerful "hello, folks" he began to say froze on his tongue when he noticed their tears.

His father spoke first.

"Donnie, we have some bad news." The rough sound

of his father's voice scared Donavan. "It's about Vic."

"What happened?" Donavan remembered rubbing his stomach, trying to calm the jittery feelings that popped up.

"Your uncle has been in a terrible accident," his mother said, and the expression on her face was the saddest Donavan had ever seen. Uncle Vic was her brother. "He's in a hospital in Germany. Grandma and I are going to see him. We leave in two days."

Donavan folded his arms across his stomach and pressed hard.

"Grandma?" He waited for an answer. His grandmother always saw the best side of anything, but this time she said nothing. He watched new tears run down her face. "Grandma, is it going to be all right?" No answer. "Grandma?" He slowly walked over to her chair and hugged her tight until his face was wet with tears too.

Donavan looked at his plate of crackers. His appetite had disappeared.

"Uncle Vic is coming to dinner Sunday," Donavan mumbled, and let out a loud, weary sigh. The last time he had seen his uncle was a hot day in August at the military rehabilitation hospital.

The grown-ups had visited Uncle Vic regularly, and

each time they came home, they had good news. His father said Uncle Vic looked healthy and had gained weight; his mother said he was laughing and talking like his old self. Grandma was the happiest of all. She could not wait to bring her son home.

In August, just before school started, his parents decided to take Donavan and Nikki to visit.

When Donavan's parents told him about the visit, he ran and told Eric and Pooh. The three of them immediately began to plan what jokes and funny stories he should tell his uncle to cheer him up.

When the day finally arrived, Donavan felt as if he had swallowed the sun. His smile was radiant. He didn't mind the long car ride. It gave him the time to practice the knock-knock jokes Pooh and Eric had helped him make up.

"Donavan," his father had said, looking in the rearview mirror, "I will pay you to quit saying those jokes."

"Why?" he asked. "I'm just trying to make sure I get them right."

"Knock, knock," his mother said.

"Who's there?" answered his father.

"Kenya," Nikki said, laughing.

"Kenya who?" his mom asked.

"Kenya gimme a dollar to buy a burger?" all three said together. It was one of the jokes Donavan had been rehearsing, one that Pooh had told him.

"Okay, guys," Donavan said. "Do you want to hear my funny stories?"

"No!" everyone shouted.

Donavan had so much to tell Uncle Vic. There were stories about school, new words from his word collection, and lots and lots of news about everything and everybody. More than a year had passed since the family had waved good-bye to Uncle Vic at the armory. It had been a long, long time not to see a favorite uncle.

"We're here! We're here!" Nikki yelled, and began clapping her hands. After his father had parked the car, Donavan jumped out and ran toward the building. He wanted to see Uncle Vic before anyone else. He wanted to be the first to say hello and hug him.

"Slow down, son," his father called after him. "You're almost there."

As they walked down the long, cool hallways of the rehab center, the staff smiled and greeted his family, but Donavan didn't answer. He was going to see Uncle Vic. Donavan didn't glance at the groups of people sitting in chairs, laughing and talking.

He ran through two swinging doors into a large,

sunny room. There were lots of windows, and sunlight touched everything in the room. Donavan looked around the room and noticed a group of people all sitting in wheelchairs.

"Hey, Champ!" The voice was behind him. Donavan smiled and whirled around. He looked and saw Uncle Vic. Uncle Vic was sitting in a wheelchair. Donavan blinked in surprise. Uncle Vic was not standing tall; he was not big; he was not himself.

The only thing Donavan recognized was his uncle's smile. He also noticed that a beard covered the bottom half of this new Uncle Vic's face. *He looks so skinny*, Donavan thought instantly.

Donavan's eyes traveled down, and he noticed that the pant legs hung limp and empty from Uncle Vic's knees. Instead of moving forward, Donavan's foot stepped backward. He knew that his uncle's legs had been hurt, but until that moment, he had not understood that they were gone.

Donavan couldn't move. Every thought in his head scrambled together. The jokes, news, and funny stories disappeared.

"Come here, Champ," Uncle Vic said, and raised his opened arms. "Git over here." It was the happy, joking sound of his laugh that moved Donavan's feet. He ran. Uncle Vic's arms closed around him.

He hugged Uncle Vic, rubbed his face against his scratchy beard, and inhaled sweet peppermint and spicy cologne. These smells belonged only to Uncle Vic Carter.

"Uncle Vic, Uncle Vic, I missed you." Donavan's voice was shaky. Slowly he realized it was a different hug, not the bear hug he was used to feeling. It did not feel strong. Donavan realized that he was bending over and not reaching up.

"Hey, Champ. Let me take a look at you." Donavan straightened and stepped back. He watched Uncle Vic look him up and down.

"Champ, I think you're going to be a tall fellow," he said, chuckling, and Donavan noticed how thin his uncle's arms were.

"Cat got your tongue?" Uncle Vic asked, still smiling.

"No" was all Donavan could say before he heard Nikki's happy screams.

"Uncle Vic, Uncle Vic!" She ran past Donavan. "He beat me here. He beat me, but I ran as fast as I could." She leaped on Uncle Vic's lap.

"Nikki!" his mother warned.

"She's fine, she's fine." Uncle Vic's voice was muffled by Nikki's hug.

Donavan stepped back to make a space for his father

and mother. He watched and wondered why he had not understood when his parents had said, "Vic's legs have been damaged beyond repair." He had not understood when they'd said, "The doctors did all they could." He should have asked questions. But not one of them had said right out, "They cut off Vic Carter's legs." He would have remembered that.

The thin, bearded man sitting in the wheelchair was not his laughing, dancing, basketball-playing Uncle Vic Carter. Not the uncle who got on the bus at the armory and announced loudly to his family, "I'll be back!" The crowd around him had laughed and laughed. That Uncle Vic had been replaced with this "almost Uncle Vic."

Donavan looked around the room uneasily and thought, *We will never be the perfect uncle-and-nephew team again.*

Donavan lifted his head from his arms and looked around. It was getting dark outside. Soon his mother would come into the kitchen, turn on the lights, and start dinner.

Donavan stood up, stretched, and thought about Sunday. Uncle Vic was coming to dinner, and Donavan was nervous. He had not seen his uncle since that hot August day in the hospital. He didn't know how he would react. He didn't know what he would say. But Sunday was coming. Donavan glanced at the clock on the wall.

I'd better go make up with Nikki, he thought. His sister never stayed angry with him long.

CHAPTER 4

HOW IT USED TO BE

"Knock, knock." Donavan looked up and saw his mom peeping into his room. "Are you busy?" she asked. "I thought you'd sleep longer; it's Saturday."

"Come in, Mom." Donavan kept doodling on the square white pad on his desk. "I woke up early. I'm just sitting here."

"I'm on my way to the market to get a few more things for tomorrow's dinner. You want anything?" She sat on his bed.

Donavan looked at the list in her hand. "Nope."

"You've been sort of quiet lately. Anything wrong?

"Nope."

"How's your math class? Everything okay?"

"Not really." He began drawing triangles.

"Your dad and I are thinking that maybe you need a tutor. We were waiting to see how you did this semester. Do you think—"

"Mom," Donavan said quickly. "Mom, do you ever feel mad about what happened to Uncle Vic?" He rushed his words; he wanted to ask before he changed his mind. The look of surprise on her face almost stopped him from saying more, but now that he'd gotten started, he couldn't stop. "What I mean is, do you ever feel like what happened to Uncle Vic was just plain wrong? Do you wish he was like he was before the war?"

His mom sighed softly. "Yes, yes, and yes. I feel all of those things. But then I feel lucky that Vic came home alive. He's my brother, and I want him to have a good life." She moved closer to Donavan. "Donnie, I know you're having a hard time."

"Mom, I don't think I acted so good the last time I saw Uncle Vic. At the hospital I sort of spaced out."

"No, Donnie, you did very well. We all knew that you were

going to be shocked the first time you saw Vic. But Grandma, Dad, and I thought both of you kids did well."

"Nikki did better," he said softly.

His mom was quiet for a few seconds. Then she said softly, "It's hard for all of us, especially Vic Carter."

"Huh?" Donavan said in surprise.

"It's hardest of all for your uncle. He lost so much. He must miss being a firefighter."

"I'll bet he wishes every day that he had his legs back," Donavan said sadly. "I know I would."

"Wishing wouldn't change a thing," his mom answered. "Son, we all have to get used to Vic this way."

"But Mom, what if we never get used to it? What if we can't stop feeling disappointed every time—?" Donavan stopped quickly. He didn't mean to say that much. It just came spilling out.

"Disappointed?" she asked, frowning. "Why disappointed? What are we talking about, son?"

"I don't know. I just wondered if he might feel disappointed about the way things turned out. I mean with people looking at him all the time." Donavan began to wish that he had not started asking questions.

"Well. People stare, because it shocks them at first, but after a while they get used to it."

"But what if they don't? What if seeing Uncle Vic only made them sad?" Donavan stopped and took a deep breath. He knew that his mom didn't think he was talking about other people. She could probably guess he was talking about himself.

"Well, Donnie, Vic Carter has lost his legs. Everyone may wish it had not happened. But it did." She kept looking at Donavan until he lifted his eyes. "And if people would give themselves a chance, they would get used to him. I just wish that people let themselves get beyond the missing legs and see that Vic is still the person he was. There's no difference."

"But Mom, there is a big difference. It's not a little thing. He's not the same." He felt anger rippling through him. Why was it so hard to explain how he felt to his mom? Why didn't she just understand?

"Vic is still smart, funny, and a person everyone loves to have around. It may be a little uncomfortable at first, but if you keep trying—"

Donavan interrupted. "Mom, I wasn't talking about me. I was just asking."

"Donavan, are we talking about you?" his mother asked quietly. "Does being around Vic make you uncomfortable?"

Donavan could hear the concern in his mother's voice, but he couldn't talk about it with her. Uncle Vic was her baby brother. Donavan looked down at the pad and began drawing large circles. "No problem. I was just asking some questions. I'm fine."

"Okay," she said. "Well, I just hope that *people* see past the chair." His mom looked at her watch. "Oh goodness, I'd better run." She leaned over and patted Donavan on the shoulder. "I'm glad we talked about this. Are you okay?"

"I'm fine, Mom. I was just wondering, that's all."

"Oh, I forgot to ask. I know I said it was just family on Sunday, but do you think Eric and Pooh might want to come over? They used to enjoy being with your uncle."

"No, Mom. They're busy," he said quickly.

His mother leaned over and gave him a hug. "See you later. And, honey, your dad wants you to help him bring some chairs up from the basement."

Donavan sat and stared out the window. He wanted to sort out the tangled thoughts in his head. Talking with his mom had just added more thoughts. He missed his uncle the old way. And he'd never really thought about how Uncle Vic must miss his old life. Uncle Vic's firefighting days were over.

But his mom was right. No matter how he felt or how Uncle Vic felt, Vic's legs were not going to come back. Donavan would have to find a new way of seeing

Uncle Vic and being with him. It would be hard because all of the things that he loved about his uncle—playing basketball, dancing, being a great firefighter—had changed. What the new way would be, he didn't know.

He looked out his window and saw his mother opening her car door. She looked up, smiled, and gave him a thumbs-up sign. He laughed and returned the sign. Nikki ran from the house carrying Breezy, her cat, in a basket. She looked up, waved, and scrambled into the backseat of the car.

Donavan wondered if Nikki missed how Uncle Vic would lift her high above his head and turn her into an airplane. Maybe she was too young to remember. He never asked her.

Tomorrow was Sunday and the family was coming to dinner to welcome Uncle Vic home from the rehab hospital for good. Donavan was going to take his mom's advice to "look past the chair." Tomorrow he would laugh and talk with his uncle. He still remembered how tongue-tied he was at the hospital. That wouldn't happen again. Sunday he would welcome Uncle Vic home.

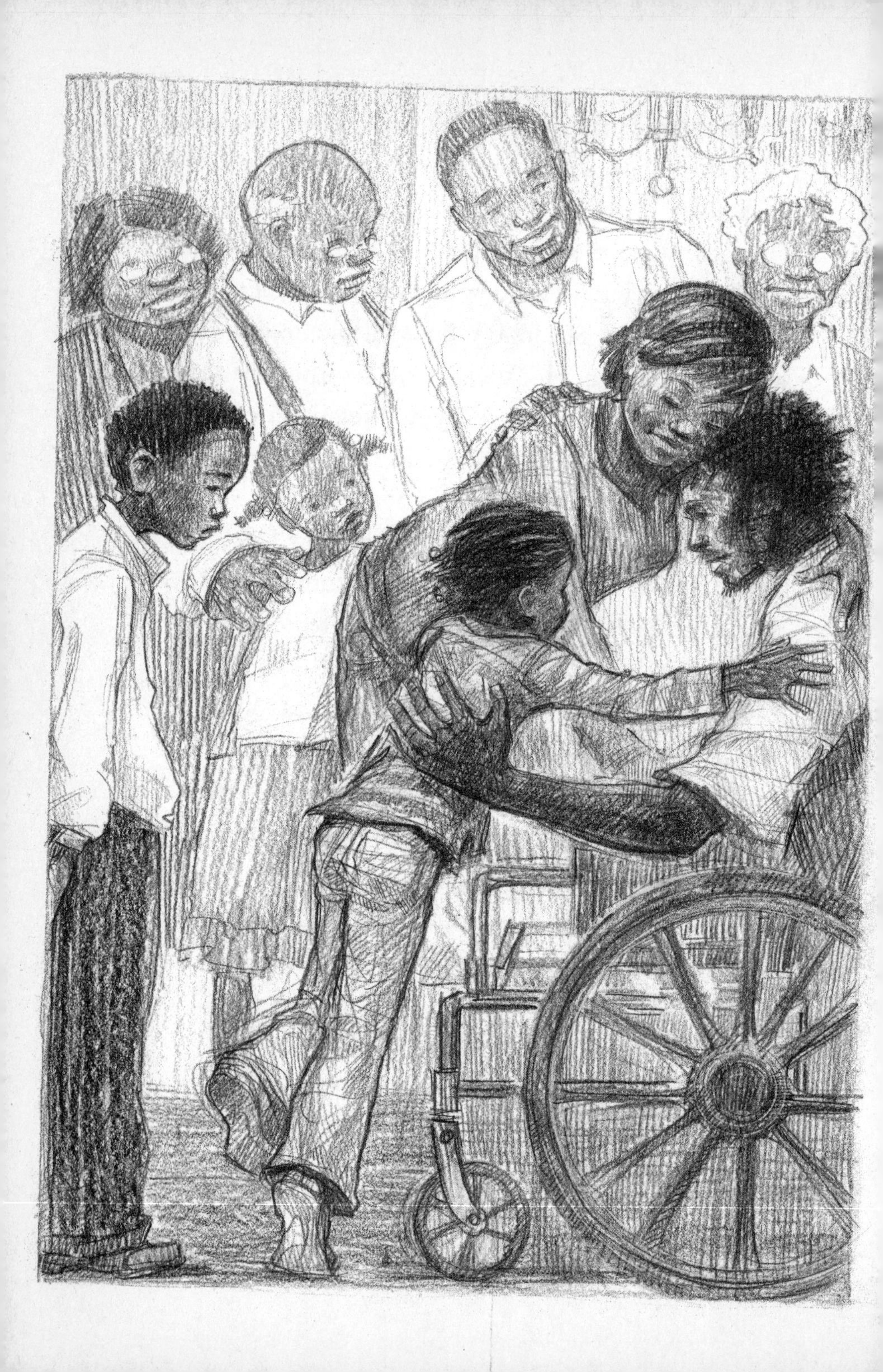

CHAPTER 5

HELLO, UNCLE VIC

"Get the door! Will someone please get the door?" Donavan heard his mother's voice over the hum of conversation in the living room.

"I'll get it!" he called, weaving a path around his grandmother and her sister, his great-aunt Weezie. They were sitting on the sofa looking at the family photo album.

"I thought Gilbert was answering the door," Aunt Weezie said, looking over her half-moon glasses.

"He went to pick up Uncle Vic." Nikki was sitting at the card table, playing checkers with Aunt Weezie's granddaughter, Vonda.

"That's probably them now." Vonda grinned at Nikki. "King me." She watched gleefully as Nikki stacked a red checker on her man.

Donavan had been thinking about this moment since his Saturday-morning talk with his mother. He was determined to overcome his feelings and be comfortable around his uncle. Inhaling deeply, he opened the door with a big smile.

"Welcome, Uncle Vic!" he said cheerfully, and looked at his uncle sitting in his chair. They were the same height.

For a moment Uncle Vic just stared, and then he mumbled, "How you doing?" His quick greeting surprised Donavan, and so did the lack of a smile on his uncle's face.

"Fine," Donavan said, and stepped back. He watched Uncle Vic guide his chair over the bump on the doorsill and roll into the living room.

"How about me?" Great-Uncle Gilbert asked, smiling. He walked behind Uncle Vic's chair carrying two bags of ice.

"Hello, Uncle Gilbert." Donavan wondered why Uncle Vic's greeting had been so short. "The gang's in the living room," he said, and closed the door. Uncle Vic always called the family "the gang."

"He's here!" Grandma announced, and everyone started talking. Donavan could hear his grandma's happy voice. "Hello, son. You're looking good."

"Vic, what took you so long?" his mother asked, moving a chair so that he could wheel near the sofa.

"Surprise!" Aunt Weezie said. "I bet you didn't expect to see me."

"Good to see you, Aunt Weezie." Uncle Vic's voice sounded soft among the loud chatter.

"Hello, Vic," Donavan's father said, waving. "Y'all let the man get in the door!" he told his relatives. "Let him take his coat off."

"Vic, I was surprised that you kept your house down the street. That's a big house," Aunt Weezie said. "I'm gonna have to come and plant flowers for you in the spring."

"Uncle Vic," Nikki asked. "Do you remember Miz Bernice? She lives next door. She told me to tell you hello. She said you used to cut her grass."

"Yes, I remember her," Vic said. Donavan wondered if anyone noticed how quiet his answers were.

"Uncle Vic, do you remember me?" Vonda asked shyly.

"I sure do. You're Aunt Weezie's granddaughter, right?"

"Right!" Vonda said. Donavan noticed that Uncle Vic was beginning to smile.

Uncle Gilbert announced, "Y'all gonna love Vic's house. It looks great. Greg, your guys really made that house accessible. Vic can move around there perfectly."

Donavan's father beamed with pride. "We've been working on it for a while. Grandma got us started. She wanted to surprise Vic when he came home."

"Vic, were you surprised?" his mom asked.

"I was flabbergasted," Uncle Vic said, and they laughed.

"Donnie, there's an excellent word for your jar," Grandma said, smiling.

Donavan watched his family in action. They each wanted to ask Uncle Vic a question. But half the time, before Uncle Vic could answer, someone made a comment and then someone else wanted to tell him gossip. *Wow*, Donavan thought, *we're a noisy bunch.*

He studied Uncle Vic carefully and noticed that he looked better than he had in August. He wasn't as skinny. His beard was shorter and his hair was longer.

"Uncle Vic," Nikki said, "your hair looks like black spaghetti." The family chuckled.

"They're called locks. My hair is locked," Uncle Vic said. "I wanted a different look."

"I think they look great!" Grandma said cheerfully.

"Me too." Aunt Weezie turned to her husband. "Gilbert, do you think you could grow locks?" she asked.

Uncle Gilbert rubbed his shaved head and smiled. "I don't think so. Maybe I could buy some." This made everyone laugh, and all the different conversations started up again.

Donavan noticed that Uncle Vic didn't ask any questions. He just looked from face to face and smiled. But his smile wasn't a Vic Carter smile, not the wide smile that could easily turn into a laugh. This smile was too polite. It was a smile for strangers. Maybe, Donavan thought, he wasn't the only one who felt uncomfortable about Vic's homecoming dinner.

"Pass the rolls," Nikki said loudly. "Would someone please pass the rolls?" Donavan reached for the basket of rolls and handed them to his father, who passed them on. Family dinners were the noisiest kind of gathering. People would dip in and out of one another's conversations until the talk sounded like a blizzard of words. His grandma was the best and her sister Aunt Weezie was second. They could be in several different conversations at once and never get confused.

His father was talking about a client who ordered a slate roof but wanted the slate orange.

"Greg, go online. I bet you'll find orange slate somewhere on the Internet," Uncle Gilbert suggested.

Grandma added, "He's right. The Internet is wonderful."

His mom was talking about a beautiful marble owl that she saw in her favorite antiques shop and wanted to buy.

"Make sure you look at that owl carefully. It may not be genuine marble," Aunt Weezie cautioned.

Nikki and Vonda were talking about Breezy, the family cat. Nikki insisted that Breezy was a tabby cat and Vonda disagreed.

Uncle Gilbert started a discussion with Vic about which varnish was best for an antique bureau.

"I used to love making old furniture look new," Uncle Vic was saying.

"I'm glad to see you working again," Uncle Gilbert commented.

Uncle Vic looked around the table. "I just hope I still have my touch."

"Of course you still have a magic touch with furniture!" Grandma exclaimed.

"Vic," Aunt Weezie said, "it's like riding a bike. You never forget."

Donavan was trying to decide which conversation he wanted to be in when his grandmother introduced the subject of Heritage Month.

"Donavan," she said, scooping a spoonful of mashed sweet potatoes onto her plate. "I hear that Grandville Coleman is coming to speak at your school. Is that true?"

Everyone at the table stopped talking and listened.

"He's coming and bringing his film about kids in South Africa." Donavan used his fork to lift a fat chicken breast from the platter in front of him. His mother reached over to put a spoonful of string beans on Donavan's plate. He looked glumly at the vegetables.

"Donavan, don't forget to taste some of my potato salad," Grandma said. The thought of her potato salad erased his frown.

"Do you think that Breezy can come to Heritage Month?" Nikki asked.

"No," Vonda said. "They don't allow animals."

"Breezy is family!" Nikki said.

"I wish we lived around here," Aunt Weezie said, pouring iced tea in Vonda's glass. "I'd love to see Grandville's new film."

"Me too," Vonda agreed. "I like School 5011."

"Goodness," Uncle Vic said, "I haven't seen Pop Grandville in years." He held his glass up for Aunt Weezie to fill. "It would be great to meet him again."

"Uncle Vic, are you coming to Heritage Month?" Nikki asked.

"What's Heritage Month, and when does it happen?" Vic asked. "When I went to School 5011, there was Black History Month. Is this a replacement?"

"Nooo!" everybody said.

"Heritage Month is in April," Donavan explained.

"It's a celebration of all of the ethnic groups in the school," Grandma explained. "Alice Cassel started it when she became principal."

"Alice Cassel is the principal?" Uncle Vic asked in surprise, and then laughed. "Well, what do you know? I took her to my senior prom."

"And she's still the second-prettiest woman I know," Donavan's father said, and winked at his wife.

Grandma continued, "Your father went several years ago. He was a big hit. Everyone loved him." The family smiled at the pride in Grandma's voice.

"Uncle Vic, maybe you could come and bring your fire engine!" Vonda said. The conversations stopped.

"He can't," Nikki said.

"Oh!" Vonda sounded disappointed.

"Vonda, Uncle Vic lost his legs in the war and he's not a firefighter anymore," Nikki explained patiently.

"But I thought you said Uncle Vic was getting new legs." Vonda looked at Uncle Vic. "Didn't you get your new legs, Uncle Vic? Aren't you as good as new? That's what Grandma Weezie said."

Donavan couldn't believe Nikki and Vonda. Horrified, he looked at his uncle. There was silence for several seconds before Uncle Vic spoke.

"I'm not a firefighter anymore." He paused and cleared his throat. "Yes, I've got my new legs, but I need to practice with them a little bit more."

No one said anything, and the quiet felt funny to Donavan. He wanted to fill it.

"Somebody's father came last year with a fire engine

and brought some old firefighting equipment," he said quickly.

"The speakers are always a big hit, but I love the exhibits," Dad said, reaching for an ear of corn. "I just wish I had something to contribute."

Donavan blinked. His father was acting like Nikki and Vonda had never said anything, and so was his mom.

"Greg, you do contribute," his mother said. "You're president of the Fathers' Club." She turned and spoke to Uncle Vic. "His club makes sure that everything runs smoothly. The maintenance workers couldn't do it without his team." His mother passed his dad the butter dish, and everyone at the table began eating and talking again.

Uncle Gilbert snapped his fingers and said, "Hey Vic, I have an excellent idea. Why don't you participate in Heritage Month? You have all of those neat little animal carvings. Maybe you could create a wooden zoo."

Grandma beamed. "Gilbert, that's a nifty idea." She looked around the table to see if everyone agreed.

"Oh, snap!" Nikki said. "I wish I'd thought of that. I like your carvings. The one you made of Breezy is beautiful."

"Yes, yes!" Donavan's mother said. "Vic, I don't know if people carve or whittle anymore. The kids would love to see what you can make out of a tiny piece of wood." Donavan's father nodded in agreement.

"Uncle Vic," Vonda said excitedly, "I'll come to see your animals."

Donavan watched Uncle Vic. He didn't seem to have the excitement that the rest of the family was showing. He didn't jump right in and make a lot of suggestions. Maybe he wasn't happy about this, just like he wasn't happy about the dinner.

"I heard Ms. Strickland say that they had too many people," Donavan said.

"Oh darn!" Vonda was disappointed.

"Oh really?" Uncle Vic bit into an ear of corn. He chewed slowly. "Well, maybe next year."

Grandma wasn't about to give up. "I'm going to write a note to Ms. Cassel and ask if she can put Vic's animal carvings on display. Donavan, I want you to take the note directly to her on Monday morning."

"What if someone steals his collection?" Donavan asked, glancing at his uncle.

"That's a point," Uncle Vic said, and winked at Donavan. Suddenly Donavan felt uncomfortable. Uncle Vic did not smile when he winked. He wondered if Uncle Vic knew that Donavan was trying to help him.

"Oh, don't worry about that," Dad said. "Things are pretty secure around School 5011." He sipped his iced tea. "Donnie, give the note to Ms. Cassel. Vic, she just might want to talk to you."

"About what?" Uncle Vic asked, and the sharpness of his voice stopped the conversation around the table. His father did not seem bothered by Vic's tone.

"Maybe she'll invite you to speak to the kids about carving and whittling. Let them know that it's an art form that's been around for years."

Donavan used his fork to push his string beans aside and wondered why the family was trying to get Uncle Vic to visit School 5011. Didn't they notice that he didn't care?

All evening Donavan had been waiting for a chance to talk to Uncle Vic alone. *Maybe after dinner*, he thought, and looked up from his plate when Uncle Gilbert cleared his throat and spoke.

"Vic, did you visit that basketball team I was telling you about?"

Donavan's fork fell from his hand and clattered on the plate. "Huh?" he asked, looking around the table.

"I've been a few times," Uncle Vic mumbled, and looked down at his plate.

"You playing ball again?" Aunt Weezie asked. "Great!"

"I played a little at the rehab center." Uncle Vic looked uneasy. "I don't know if I want to keep doing it." Donavan noticed that the adults at the table didn't jump in and start talking at once. They seemed to be waiting. Uncle Vic looked at the faces around the table. "I don't know if I like wheelchair basketball. I just don't know." He sighed. The sound wasn't happy. Then he bent his head and began eating. "Mom," he said, "your potato salad is still great."

The adults at the table began talking about who was the best cook in the family. Donavan stopped listening to the chatter and thought about what Uncle Vic had just said. Wheelchair basketball. *Ugh!* And Aunt Weezie had said, "Great!" *Duh*, he thought. *Wrong answer.* What could be great about basketball in a wheelchair?

Donavan shook his head in disgust. He didn't blame Uncle Vic for not wanting to play. After being a great basketball player, why would he want to dribble or shoot from a wheelchair?

"What does wheelchair basketball even look like?" Donavan didn't realize he had said his thoughts aloud until his father called his name.

"Donavan! What did you say?" His father's expression was serious.

Donavan focused on the surprised looks on the faces around the table. Before he could think of an answer, his Uncle Vic spoke.

"It looks different. Instead of players running around, they are wheeling around."

"I think I'd like to see that." Grandma's voice was cheery.

"You won't see me playing." Uncle Vic's voice was firm. "In fact," he said, reaching for the bowl of potato salad, "I want to talk about something else." He spooned some salad onto his plate and then reached over to put a spoonful on Donavan's.

"Thanks," Donavan mumbled, and wished he could disappear in a puff of smoke. He didn't care where he went, as long as it wasn't at the family dinner table. He hoped he hadn't hurt Uncle Vic's feelings. Donavan looked up and was surprised to see his uncle staring at him with an expression that Donavan did not understand. He smiled shyly at Uncle Vic and began to eat his potato salad.

CHAPTER 6

HELPING UNCLE VIC

Monday mornings at School 5011 are crazy, Donavan thought. *It's like everyone forgets what to do over the weekend.* He followed Nikki to her classroom, carrying a large, cardboard box.

"This is heavy," he complained, walking into the classroom. "Where do I put it?"

Nikki pointed to a large banner that hung over a table in the back of the classroom. "Science Projects," she read aloud, and walked to the table. "We're the first ones here."

Donavan placed the box down carefully. "Oomph!" Lifting the flap, he peeped inside. "Everything looks great. Nothing spilled out. Nikki?" He looked at her. It wasn't like Nikki to be so quiet. "Are you nervous?"

"I'm a little bit nervous, but it's going away." She lifted the flap. "It's perfect. You carried it just right. Let's take it out."

They lifted a round bowl from the box and set it on the table. Nikki pulled a poster from the box and placed it beside the bowl. She examined everything carefully. "I sure hope no one else has a terrarium."

"Don't worry, Nikki. Even if they do, yours will be the best." He patted Nikki on the back and headed for the door. Several of Nikki's classmates came into the classroom with their science projects. "Hey, Nikki, good luck."

"Thanks! And Donnie, don't forget to give Ms. Cassel Grandma's note," Nikki called, not looking away from her terrarium.

"I won't," Donavan promised, and hurried down the hall to the principal's office.

Usually Donavan didn't mind going there. He enjoyed watching the students bustling in and out and listening to the crackly announcements coming from the intercom. But this morning he didn't think going to see Ms. Cassel was the best idea. He had his grandmother's note for her in his backpack.

Donavan had never found time to talk to his uncle alone on Sunday, but he'd watched Uncle Vic carefully and noticed that he did not move around much. Once he put his chair in a spot, he stayed there. He joined in a couple of the board games, but he didn't laugh or make jokes. Most of the evening Uncle Vic sat smiling and watching. He answered questions but never asked any. He had never been so quiet and softspoken before.

Miz Utz's cheery voice startled him. "Hello, word gatherer."

"Morning," he replied, and stood at the counter to wait until she finished talking on the phone and writing on a slip of paper. Several second graders were ahead of him; they'd lost their lunch tickets. Donavan looked on the counter and saw a stack of flyers bundled in clear plastic wrap. They were for Heritage Month.

Miz Utz handed three of the students green lunch tickets. "Don't lose them," she warned. "Kids, go straight to your homeroom." Donavan pulled his gaze from the flyers and smiled. He'd almost forgotten his excellent idea about being a greeter.

"What can I do for you, Donavan?" Miz Utz asked.

Donavan hesitated for a moment. "Miz Utz, have a lot of students signed up to be greeters for Heritage Month?"

Miz Utz pulled a yellow pad from under the counter and looked at it. "No, there are only two names on the list." She frowned. "I think I'll ask the fifth-grade teachers to make an announcement."

"Well, do you think I could sign up?" Donavan asked.

"Greeters have to be in the fifth grade," Miz Utz said.

"But I'm almost in fifth," Donavan argued. "In six months I'll pass to the fifth."

Miz Utz laughed. "Young man, you can have this discussion with Ms. Cassel." The school intercom buzzed and Miz Utz answered it. Donavan began to think about how he could convince Ms. Cassel to let him join the greeters.

Miz Utz covered the mouthpiece of the phone with her hand. "Donavan, how can I help you?"

"Can I speak to Ms. Cassel for a moment?"

"She's in her office. You'd better hurry. Class starts in five minutes." Miz Utz began paging someone.

Donavan knocked on Ms. Cassel's door and waited. He listened. Not a sound, so he cracked the door. "Ms. Cassel?" he called. No answer. He opened the door wider and slipped inside.

"Hello?" he called louder, looking around the room. Donavan began planning what he would say. *Maybe I should just ask for me and then let Eric and Pooh speak for themselves. Or maybe,* he thought, *after she lets me join, I'll tell her about Eric and Pooh.*

Donavan looked down at Ms. Cassel's desk and

noticed the rows and piles of papers. He admired the tall plants on the windowsills, the golden trophies that sat on shelves, and the colorful posters that hung on the walls. He looked at a cartoon map of the city and snickered at a drawing of the mayor sitting on top of City Hall. He had moved closer to see if School 5011 was on the map when he heard a swishing, rustling sound behind him.

"I thought I heard a sound out here," Ms. Cassel said, walking out of a large closet. "Good morning, Donavan. How may I help you?"

"Good morning. Miz Utz said I could come and ask you a question."

"Okay."

"Miz Utz said only two fifth graders signed up to be greeters. And we always need lots of greeters for Heritage Month. So I was wondering if I could be one." He expelled a breath of relief. He got it all out and it sounded right.

"Ummm." Ms. Cassel squinted her eyes. It looked like she was thinking. "I thought that only fifth graders were greeters."

"Why?" Donavan asked.

Ms. Cassel raised an eyebrow in surprise. "Why? Well, because they are the seniors of the school. And . . ."

"Ms. Cassel, I'm almost a senior. I will be next year,

and this year is almost over. In two weeks it will be March, and Heritage Month is in April and then there's May and in June I'll pass to the fifth grade." He folded his arms across his chest and smiled.

"It's still February, and more fifth graders may sign up," Ms. Cassel said, shaking her head. "Why don't you check back in March and see if more fifth graders sign up? How does that sound?" She looked at the clock.

"Aw, come on, Ms. Cassel, please. I want to be a greeter and I think I could do a good job. I've been watching the greeters since I was in the third grade. And I—"

Ms. Cassel interrupted. "Donavan, I'll put your name on a wait list. That way I'll remember that you asked first. But the fifth graders get preference. Understand?"

Donavan nodded. "Yes."

Ms. Cassel looked at the clock again. "It's almost time for the bell. You don't want to be late for class." She walked to the door. "Anything else?" she asked.

"No," Donavan said.

"Cheer up." Ms. Cassel was smiling. "There are lots of jobs to do during Heritage Month."

"But Ms. Cassel, I want to do something important," Donavan said stubbornly.

Ms. Cassel laughed. "Donavan, every job is important."

Donavan stopped suddenly as he remembered. "Oh,

Ms. Cassel, my grandmother wanted to know if you had space for another display during Heritage Month."

"Oh, I don't know. I'll have to check with Ms. Strickland. She's in charge of the display cases. Do you know why your grandmother is interested?"

"Yes, she wanted to display my uncle Vic's carvings."

"Tell your grandmother I'll call her tomorrow afternoon. I'm so busy today I can't squeeze a thing on my calendar." Ms. Cassel gently nudged Donavan out the door. "Your grandmother should get in touch with me if she doesn't hear anything in a few days."

Donavan remembered what his uncle had said about Ms. Cassel and his prom. "Ms. Cassel, do you remember Vic Carter Johnson?"

She was silent for several moments. He could tell by her expression that she was thinking.

"He's my uncle," Donavan added.

"Vic Carter, Vic Carter." Ms. Cassel's expression was thoughtful. "My goodness, I haven't heard that name in years." She laughed. "Donavan, I do know your uncle. Didn't he play all-star basketball in high school and college?"

"Yes, I think so." Donavan nodded. "But—"

"Indeed, I do remember Vic Carter Johnson. He was the tallest boy in high school, he ran track, and he was the best dancer. In fact," Ms. Cassel said, "I wonder if he remembers that he took me to our senior prom. How is your uncle?"

"He's not—he's not like he use to be, he was hurt," Donavan said quietly. Ms. Cassel did not say anything. She just looked at him as if she was waiting for him to continue. He licked his lips. "I think he's doing better. But he doesn't go out much."

"I'm sorry to hear that he's been injured. When you see him, tell him I said hello," Ms. Cassel said.

"I'll tell him," Donavan answered.

"You'd better get a move on. Classes are starting." Ms. Cassel smiled. "How is your math class?"

"It's okay. I'm trying to do better." He noticed his backpack leaning against the counter and picked it up.

"Keep trying," she said. "And Donavan, don't forget to tell your uncle I said hello." She paused and then added, "He may not remember me."

"He remembers you. See you, Ms. Cassel." He waved to Miz Utz as he stepped into the noisy hall.

Man oh man, he thought. How would Ms. Cassel react if she saw his uncle Vic? She only remembered him dancing and running and playing basketball. He couldn't tell her that Uncle Vic had lost his legs.

The loud sound of the bell jolted Donavan from his thoughts. He ran to get to homeroom and tried to shake thoughts of Uncle Vic out of his mind. The day was starting off right. He had helped Nikki deliver her science project, his name was going on the wait list for greeters, and at lunchtime he would let Eric and Pooh know.

He didn't give a thought to Grandma's note for Ms. Cassel, still inside his backpack.

CHAPTER 7

HOW ABOUT A VISIT?

I've been looking forward to today all week." Donavan leaned closer to the game board.

"Me too. We haven't hung out together in a long time," Eric said, watching the board.

"I wonder what happened to Pooh." Donavan reached for a domino.

"I don't know." Eric frowned. "It's Saturday morning. Maybe he overslept."

"Maybe." Donavan took his turn. "If he doesn't come soon, he's gonna miss half the day. Besides, I wanted to talk about Heritage Month and us being greeters."

"You think that's gonna happen?" Eric sat back in his

chair to study what Donavan laid down.

"What did Miz Utz say when you guys signed up?" Donavan asked.

"Nothing." Eric chewed his bottom lip and concentrated on his next move. The boys had planned this Saturday for weeks; they were going to spend the whole day hanging out. Eric had arrived early and eaten breakfast with Donavan and his family. Now the two boys were playing dominoes in the family room and waiting for Pooh.

"Wow!" Donavan looked at the table in surprise as Eric laid down his last domino. "Three games! I can't believe you won three games in a row."

"Believe it." Eric rubbed his hands together gleefully.

Donavan saw the smug expression on Eric's face and knew his friend would be bragging forever.

"I'm getting better and better," Eric said proudly. "Boy, I'm beating you like a drum."

"You're lucky. I was thinking about something else," Donavan grumbled.

"Stop worrying. We're either going to be greeters or get a different job," Eric said.

"But being greeters would be just too cool," Donavan argued. "Nobody else in the fourth grade has ever been a greeter. Think about it."

Eric laughed and made his voice deep. "We're going

where no fourth grader has gone before."

Donavan copied Eric's voice. "To a galaxy filled with excitement and adventure!" He started to say more, but he heard a knock on the door. "Who's there?" he called out.

A faint voice said, "Knock, knock."

"Who's there?" Donavan called louder.

"Owl," the muffled voice answered.

"Owl who?"

"Owl be here until you open the door."

Donavan let his friend in. "Get in here, Pooh. I knew it was you the minute I heard 'knock, knock,'" he said, laughing.

"It could've been someone else," Pooh objected.

"Nah," Donavan said. "No one else is in love with knock-knock jokes like you."

Pooh was carrying a wooden box. "Who's losing?" he asked, looking at Eric.

"I'm not on my best game," Donavan explained. "I'm thinking about us being greeters for Heritage Month."

"Yeah, right," Eric boasted. "That's his excuse 'cause I am whipping poor Donnie like batter."

"Eric, give it a rest," Donavan complained. "You're stuck on bragging."

"I'm not just bragging. I'm winning!" Eric declared, beating his chest.

Donavan ignored him and turned to Pooh. "When

you guys signed up, what did Miz Utz say? Were there more than two names on the list? You think we've got a shot at being greeters?"

Pooh held up his hand to stop the questions. "Miz Utz said, 'You boys are pretty adamant about being greeters.' And I said, 'We sure are,' and then I asked her if she thought we had a chance and she said, 'Maybe,' and that's all she said."

"That sounds okay," Donavan said. "At least she didn't say we had no chance."

"Oh yeah," Pooh said. "She said, 'Good luck, guys.' And I didn't see the fifth-grade list, only the wait list. And the only names on that list are ours."

"Okay, sounds good." Donavan was satisfied. "What's that you've got?"

"It's an old wooden box I found in our basement. My moms said it belonged to Pop Grandville. I want to keep my valuables in it. You never know, the things I collect may be worth a lot someday." Pooh placed the box on the table.

Donavan leaned closer. "It looks like someone forgot to throw it away."

"True, true," Eric said, looking over Pooh's shoulder. "The top is all busted and cracked, and it's really scratched, but it's a nice size for storing stuff."

"And it's big," Pooh added. "And I like the velvet on

the inside. Moms said I should take it to your uncle Vic. She says he likes fixing things."

"My uncle Vic?" Donavan asked, surprised. "You remember him?" He hadn't mentioned his uncle since last summer, when Pooh and Eric had helped him come up with jokes to welcome Uncle Vic home. A few times they'd asked about his visit to the rehab center. Donavan gave them short answers: "fine," "okay," and "all right." After a while they stopped asking.

Pooh explained. "I really don't remember him that well, but my moms said he was good at fixing old things. She said he restored our dining-room chairs. My dad said when he saw the chairs they looked new again."

"I haven't seen your uncle in a long time. It would be cool to see him again. I remember he made us laugh," Eric said.

"He was always so much fun." Pooh turned from the table and dribbled an imaginary ball around the room. "He had the smoothest hook shot I ever seen." Pooh bent his knees and pretended to shoot a basket. "Bam!" he said, leaping in the air. Eric and Pooh laughed.

"That was a long time ago," Donavan snapped. "He doesn't do that anymore."

Pooh looked surprised. "I

know that, but man, he was good when he was playing."

"He's still good." Donavan's voice was harsh.

"I came around to see if you would walk to his house with me. I don't want to go there alone." Pooh sounded puzzled.

"Why?" Donavan asked suspiciously. "What do you think my uncle would do to you?"

"What could he do to me?" Pooh asked angrily. "It's just that I haven't seen him since he lost his legs, and . . ." Pooh looked around uneasily.

"My uncle is not some freak that you have to be afraid of!" Donavan shouted.

Eric dropped the box top he was holding. "Hey! Hey!" he said, pushing his way in between Donavan and Pooh.

"What you talking about? I definitely ain't afraid of your uncle Vic!" Pooh shouted. "Why are you acting so weird?"

"I don't want you going around my uncle just to see what he looks like now. He's different. He's not a dancing, running, jumping basketball player." Donavan's words poured out of his mouth in an angry stream.

"Stop it, guys!" Eric commanded. "Donnie, calm down. Pooh, apologize."

"For what!" Pooh shouted, and pushed Eric aside. "Apologize for what?" His face was inches from Donavan's. "I am *not* afraid of your uncle. I just don't know what to say to him because I haven't seen him in so long." He took a deep breath and lowered his voice. "I thought it would be fun for all of us to go and try to decide what he could do with my box. My moms said that he had a lot of real neat things in his garage." Pooh waited a few seconds. "Why would I think your uncle was a freak? I like your uncle Vic a lot."

"Donnie, stop acting crazy," Eric said. "We're buddies. Nobody thinks your uncle is a freak. When he lost his legs, we felt sad. You never talk about him, so we don't bring it up." Eric was looking at Donavan as if he had two heads.

Donavan stepped back. Embarrassment fizzed through his body. He scratched his head and lowered his eyes. The expression on Pooh's face shamed him; Eric's confused look added to his misery. Donavan opened his mouth to speak and then closed it quickly. He didn't know what to say.

"I would never laugh at anybody in a wheelchair." Pooh's voice sounded almost tearful.

"You know you're wrong," Eric said accusingly to Donavan.

"I know" was all that Donavan could say. "I—I—I . . ." He stopped. He couldn't find the right words to say how wrong he had been. So he just stood there.

Eric came to the rescue. "Hey, why don't we all go over to Uncle Vic's, 'cause if we stay here, I'm gonna have to whip both of y'all in a game of dominoes." He laughed at his own joke. "I'm just that good."

"Dream on." Donavan glanced quickly at Pooh.

"Are we going?" Eric asked. "We might find something interesting."

"I dunno," Pooh mumbled. He wasn't smiling.

"Knock, knock," Donavan said. Pooh didn't answer.

"Knock, knock," Donavan said louder.

"Who's there?" Pooh asked reluctantly.

"Don't chew," Donavan responded.

"Don't chew who?" Pooh asked, biting his lip to keep from grinning.

"Don't chew wanna go treasure hunting?" Donavan asked with a big grin and was relieved to see his friend smiling at him.

"Yeah, let's go," Pooh said, and reached for his box. "But the last one there has to carry the winner home."

"On his back!" Donavan added gleefully. They ran for the door.

CHAPTER 8

HANGING OUT AT UNCLE VIC'S

Victory goes to the greatest!" Donavan shouted, running toward the gate of Uncle Vic's yard, his arms raised over his head. "Hey, Eric, get ready to carry me all the way home!"

"I'm second!" Pooh shouted. He was running and still carrying his wooden box.

"Yeah, yeah, yeah," Eric grumbled as he leaned against the fence. "You guys bunched up and I couldn't pass y'all," he complained.

The sudden, loud sound of dogs barking startled the boys. "Whoa!" Eric shouted, and moved quickly away from the gate. Two large shaggy dogs, one black and one gray, jumped against the other side of the fence.

"Down, boys! Down, boys!" Donavan tried to make his voice sound deep and firm. "Mutt, Jeff, get down!"

"We better not go in yet," Pooh said. Eric nodded in agreement. "Those dogs look mean." The boys took several steps backward and eyed the dogs cautiously.

"They're okay." Donavan opened the gate slightly and slipped inside. "You guys wait here until I find my uncle." He held out his hand for the dogs to sniff. They ignored him and kept barking, but they no longer looked or sounded threatening. "They know me," Donavan said halfheartedly.

"They're not acting like it," Eric said.

"Hey, hey, what's all the sound and fury about?" The sound of Uncle Vic's voice startled Donavan. He turned and saw Vic wheeling toward him along a cement walkway. "What's up, Donnie?" Uncle Vic asked. "This is a surprise. What brings you to my backyard?"

Donavan forced his eyes up to Uncle Vic's smiling face. "I, we, we . . ." Donavan began. Suddenly he felt nervous.

"When did you start to stutter?" Uncle Vic asked, wheeling closer.

"I guess I should have called, but I just didn't think . . ."

"What brings you my way?" his uncle asked again.

"You haven't been around here"—Uncle Vic paused—"in a long time."

Donavan shifted his weight from one foot to the other. There was no anger in Uncle Vic's voice. But he wasn't smiling anymore.

Donavan wished he had called first. He would have if he hadn't acted so dumb toward Pooh. Before, Donavan could bring his buddies to Uncle Vic's house without calling. He was always welcome. *But maybe now,* he thought, *Uncle Vic wants to be alone.* Donavan wasn't sure if he'd done something wrong or not. He couldn't think because of the barking dogs.

"You still growing a beard?" he asked, because he couldn't think of anything else to say.

"Yup. I hate shaving." Uncle Vic peered around Donavan to see why the dogs were still running and barking. "Mutt, Jeff, pipe down." Immediately the dogs quieted, ran over, and started sniffing and licking Donavan's fingers. Startled, he jerked his hand away.

"Stand still," Uncle Vic ordered. "Donnie, they're just trying to get your scent. It's been a while."

"I know," Donavan answered guiltily. He stood still while Mutt and Jeff sniffed and licked him. "I think they still remember me." He patted the dogs on their heads. "They seem happy to see me." He laughed as Mutt jumped up to tickle Donavan's neck with his slippery tongue. "I missed Mutt and Jeff."

"Are those your bodyguards?" Uncle Vic asked, and gestured toward the gate. "Hey, guys, come in, come in. Mutt and Jeff won't bother you."

"Oh." Donavan turned. "I forgot. Come on in, y'all."

Pooh and Eric opened the gate and slipped in. They kept their eyes on the two dogs.

"Do you remember Pooh and Eric?" Donavan asked. "They sort of still remember you." Donavan watched the boys approach his uncle and wondered if they would be shocked. He did not know if they had ever seen a person without legs. The dogs began running around and barking excitedly again. Pooh and Eric slowed their steps.

"Just let them get your scent, boys. They won't hurt you. Come in, come and let me look at you. Mutt, Jeff, come here." Uncle Vic patted the dogs on their heads.

Uncle Vic wheeled his chair around to face the boys. Pooh and Eric waited until the dogs inspected them before they began to walk closer. Donavan watched their faces and saw their eyes widen.

Uncle Vic's smile remained friendly while Eric and Pooh looked at him. Eric stared as if he didn't understand what he was seeing. He shifted his gaze down quickly.

Pooh's mouth opened in a circle of surprise. "Man oh man," he said softly, and then clamped his lips together tightly, but he kept his eyes fixed on Uncle Vic.

Eric couldn't keep his eyes in one place; he kept looking around the yard. "I haven't been here in a long time. Where did all the grass go?" he asked, rubbing the back of his neck.

"It's hard to wheel my chair over grass, so I decided to make a big cement path. I left enough grass for Mutt and Jeff." Uncle Vic rubbed the dogs around their necks.

"Oh," Eric said, and walked closer to Uncle Vic. "Your chair is cool." He pointed to the wheels. "Is it a sports chair? I saw a chair just like this on TV. A sports show." Before Eric could continue, Pooh interrupted. He nudged Eric aside.

"Uncle, I mean Mr. Uncle Vic Carter. I—I was sorry to hear about your legs."

Donavan rolled his eyes. Pooh always said just what he thought. He held his breath and wondered if Uncle Vic was embarrassed. But then Donavan realized that his uncle didn't look uncomfortable.

"Thank you, son, but that's 'Uncle Vic,' not 'Mr. Uncle.'" His smile was welcoming.

"Yeah, sorry, Vic, I mean Uncle," Pooh said, shaking his head. "We—we were upset when Donavan told us." He stopped. "Weren't we, Eric?"

"Ah, yes," Eric said. "Yes, we were, and we—we got mad." Eric began to examine the chair again. "Why do you have a sports wheelchair?"

Donavan looked at the chair and realized it was different from the one his uncle had used on Sunday. The arms were lower and the seat was raised. His uncle was wearing a faded T-shirt and a pair of sweatpants that were tucked neatly under his thighs.

When Vic did not answer, Donavan thought he had not heard the question. But finally he replied, "I use it when I exercise." Vic glanced quickly at Donavan. "It's built for speed. I can move and turn faster in this chair."

Eric opened his mouth to ask another question, but Pooh interrupted. "We're not weird," Pooh said. "We're just nervous."

Uncle Vic chuckled loudly. "No, no, don't be nervous. It's okay."

Donavan noticed that his uncle looked at ease. And it seemed like Pooh and Eric were starting to relax as well. "Hey, Mr. Vic," Eric said, looking at Vic this time. "You remember us?"

"Umm, now let me see." Uncle Vic looked directly at the boys and stroked his beard. They giggled at the serious expression on his face.

"Yeah, yeah. I knew I recognized the two of you." He pointed to Eric and Pooh. "You were the boys who, along with *another* boy"—he looked at Donavan—"glued my basketball, the one signed by Magic Johnson, to the front porch."

"Err."

"Ahhh."

"Umm."

Each boy stammered and then laughed. Uncle Vic grinned at their surprised expressions. The dogs joined in the excitement and began to bark.

"Uncle Vic, that was so long ago. We'd forgotten that happened," Donavan said.

"We were little kids then." Eric snickered.

"Ain't no way we would do anything like that today," Pooh said, trying to look serious, but he began to laugh again after a few seconds.

"It's good seeing you fellows again. What brings you here?" Uncle Vic asked again. This time he was wearing a big smile.

Donavan explained, "Pooh had something he wanted you to look over and see if it was worth saving." Pooh ran over to the gate and grabbed the box propped against the fence. He set it on the ground in front of Uncle Vic. "I found this in my basement. My moms said it was my grandfather's when he was my age."

"You're kidding. This box belonged to Pop Grandville?" Uncle Vic grinned.

"Yup, and it's a great box, but it's pretty beat up. I want to save it. Do you think it's worth it?" Pooh asked.

"I think most things are worth saving." Uncle Vic examined the box. "I tell you what, why don't we take this down to my workshop and look it over?" Uncle Vic turned his chair. Pooh, Eric, and Donavan followed him down a ramp and under the porch into the basement.

After that first brief, awkward moment, his friends were laughing and joking with Vic. If they were uncomfortable, it didn't show. Donavan wondered why they were okay with the new Uncle Vic, and he still felt a little uneasy.

"Awesome! Cool!" Donavan could hear the excitement in his friends' voices as they explored the basement workshop.

"This is different!" Donavan exclaimed. The last time he'd been in the basement, it had held a hodgepodge of broken things. Uncle Vic had always collected neat stuff and said that he was going to fix it all one day. "One day" never came, because he was too busy being a firefighter.

But today the basement was as neat as a department store in the mall.

"Look at these tools!" Eric said, standing next to a wall covered with a large, brown pegboard. Tools of every shape, size, and function hung from clips attached to the board.

His uncle noticed Donavan's surprised expression. "Your father, Uncle Gilbert, and several of the firefighters I used to work with pitched in and redesigned the basement for me."

"I remember Uncle Gilbert talking about it at last Sunday's dinner. Everything looks good." Donavan was impressed.

Pooh held up a long pole with a clamp on the end. "Donnie, look, Uncle Vic can reach anything with this." He began waving the tool around and snapping it open and shut.

Eric was standing on a large wooden disc. "Hey, Donnie." He spun around several times.

Donavan ran over. "What the heck is this?" he asked.

"It looks like a turntable," Eric said.

"It is," Uncle Vic said. "I put furniture and other things I want to paint on it. That way I can paint without having to move the piece around."

"That's cool," Eric said, spinning faster.

"You guys settle down," Uncle Vic ordered. "I don't want anything broken."

"Donavan," Eric said, shaking his head. "Come over here and look at this old spinning wheel. I'll bet my grandmother would love this."

"Don't play with that," Uncle Vic warned. "The wheel is broken."

"Donavan, you been holding out on us?" Pooh asked. "You didn't tell us your uncle had such a great basement!" Pooh lifted the shade of a lamp shaped like a fish.

Donavan shrugged his shoulders. "I haven't been

here in a long time."

Uncle Vic interrupted. "Fellows, don't blame Donavan. It hasn't been remodeled long and I don't let just anyone roam around down here."

Donavan watched as Uncle Vic studied the tools on the pegboard for a moment and then reached over and seized a pair of pliers.

"A lot of these things belong to my new customers. I'm repairing them." Uncle Vic wheeled his chair around and smoothly pulled up to a long counter. Donavan noticed how easily he moved from place to place. Vic reached overhead and pulled a cord that hung from the ceiling, and bright light flooded the work area. "Pooh," he said, "bring that box over here."

Pooh placed the box in the light and then stood back and waited. The boys watched Vic lift the lid and examine it. He twisted and turned the box, inspecting it from every angle, and made comments like "Great wood" and "It's deep inside" and "It needs new hinges."

Donavan looked over the tools on the wall. He knew he could fill several word jars with tool words alone. Uncle Vic had everything in this room: African masks, empty picture frames, an old butter churn, two sewing machines that looked older than his grandma. He noticed a stack of wood in a corner and walked over. As he came closer, he recognized the objects—a pile of legs.

Stacked neatly were legs from chairs, tables, and other types of furniture. Donavan stared and wondered. *Why,* he thought, *are these legs put away in a corner?* Why was his uncle saving them? He didn't know what to think.

Eric walked behind him and whispered, "Boo!" Donavan flinched.

"What in the mighty-mighty?" Eric asked, looking down.

"It's a pile of broken furniture legs," Donavan said softly. "Why would he want a bunch of broken legs around?"

"I dunno," Eric said, and shrugged.

"Hey, guys!" Pooh called. "We have some ideas."

"Great!" Eric tugged at Donavan's arm. "Come on." He went to join Pooh and Uncle Vic in the discussion of how to fix the box.

Donavan looked at the pile of legs and shrugged. Maybe he would ask his dad what he thought of Uncle Vic's strange collection. "I'm coming," he said, and turned to join the group.

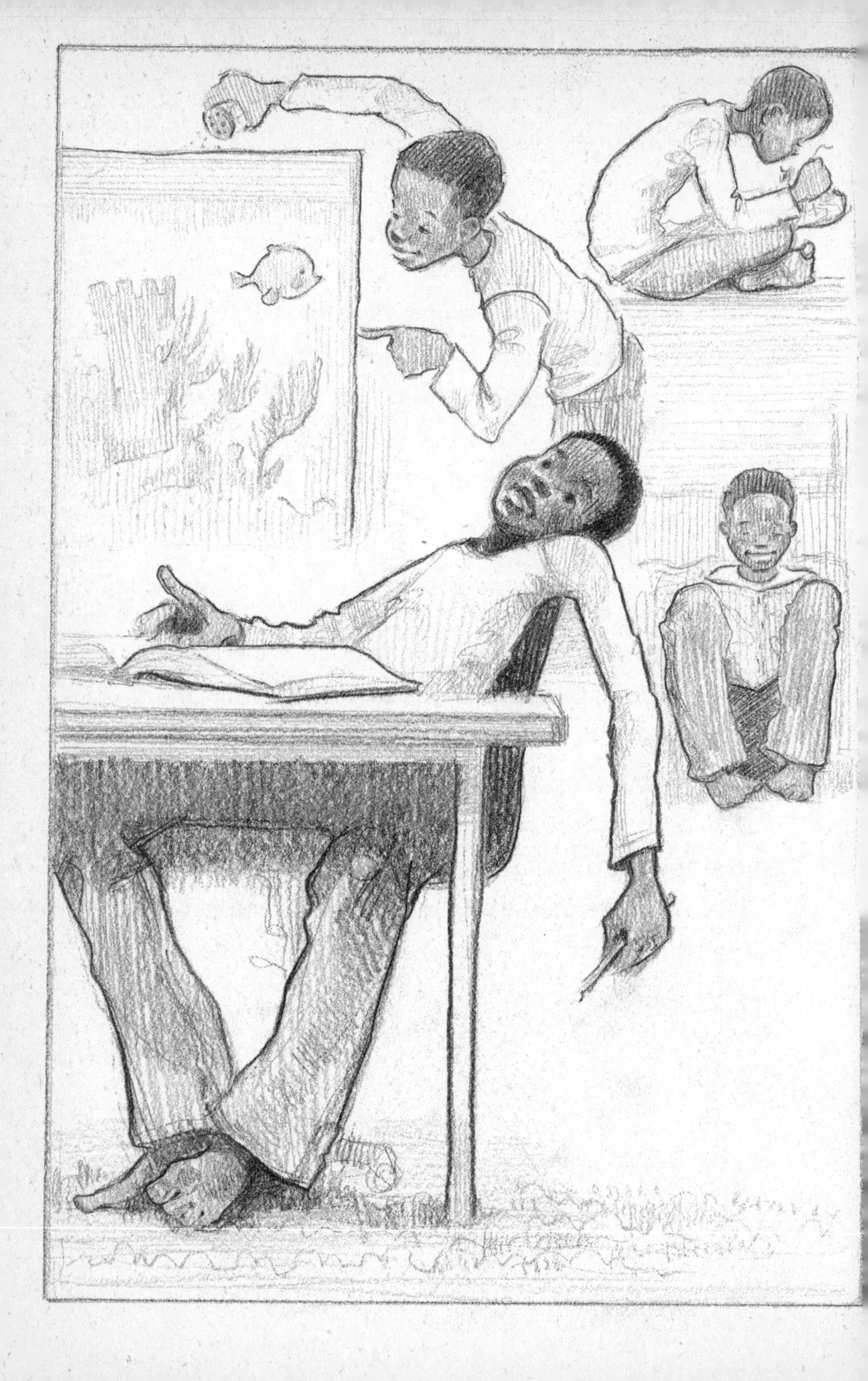

CHAPTER 9

HAVING A STRATEGY

Donavan saw his father walking past the family room. "Hey, Dad! Where you going?"

His father came in. "I didn't know you were here." He looked at the table and saw Donavan's textbook, notebook, pencils, and several sheets of paper scattered about. "It seems like you're starting the week off right. Monday evening, and you're doing some serious studying!" His father sat on the edge of the table and looked down at the papers.

"I'm trying." Donavan leaned back in the chair and tried to distract his father from looking at his homework. "What's up? You looked like you were in a hurry."

"I'm on my way over to your uncle Vic's house. I'm

gonna help him with a small project. What's this?" he asked, bending down and picking a small wad of paper from the floor.

Donavan remembered the quiz and slumped in his chair. "That was just an old quiz. It's not a test." Again he tried to change the subject. "My buddies and I went to Uncle Vic's on Saturday. We had a great time."

His father grinned. "Vic told me. That was mighty nice of you guys."

Donavan sat up in the chair. "We had a blast. And guess what, Dad?" He rushed on. "Uncle Vic decided to help Pooh rebuild his treasure chest."

"I'm glad you guys went to visit, especially you. I know how close you were to your uncle. I was beginning to worry a little, but it looks as if you're feeling comfortable, if you took your friends around Vic."

"I wasn't uncomfortable," Donavan mumbled.

His father began unfolding the paper. "Gee whiz," he said, raising an eyebrow in surprise.

Donavan was silent. He quickly looked away from his father and glanced around the room. His scalp felt tight and prickly. Donavan shifted his eyes back to his father's face while he was still examining the quiz.

His father was a good listener, but he wasn't a talkative person, so sometimes it was hard for Donavan to know what he thought. Donavan never heard him complain or saw him angry or hassled in any way. It made Donavan feel safe and secure that his father was always so calm. He wished he could be more like his dad. How great would it be if he never got bothered or upset about math?

His father cleared his throat. “Son, sometimes it’s hard to stand up to your fears. But you have to face what makes you uncomfortable. If you don’t, believe me, fears and insecurities don’t disappear. They just grow larger. Do you understand me?”

Donavan nodded.

He continued. “I know Vic’s accident was rough on you. I’ve known Vic all my life. He’s a great person. It’s very hard for me to get adjusted to Vic Carter in a wheelchair.” His father went on. “It’s tough to get things right, especially when you feel as if everyone is watching you or judging you. Am I right?”

“Yes, it’s hard.” Donavan chewed on his bottom lip. “I didn’t want anyone to think bad about me, or be mad because I didn’t want to be around Uncle Vic.” He asked softly, “Dad, are you disappointed in me?”

“Absolutely not, son!” his father said quickly. “I’m concerned. It seems to me that you’re having a rough time lately. You’ve always struggled with math, but you’ve pulled through. I saw you struggling with your feelings about your uncle Vic. I thought it was a natural reaction. I also thought you'd adjust. But I can't help wondering if you're getting a bit overwhelmed."

"I'm fine," Donavan said.

"Every time your mother and I ask you about how things are going, you say things are okay. Donnie, I've noticed that you don't always like to tackle things that are hard." He looked at Donavan and then at the wrinkled paper and said, "Trying is half the battle. I think that if you continue to visit your uncle, you'll feel more comfortable with him."

"I *am* getting used to Uncle Vic," Donavan pointed out. "And on Saturday I had a good time. It was almost like the old days,"

"Then let's focus on this." His father laid the crumpled quiz on the desk. "Math is important. It comes easy for some, but many, many people have to work extra hard to understand math."

"Why?" Donavan asked, frowning. "Why are numbers so hard for me? No matter how much I try, math is always impossible to understand. I hate going to Mr. Sullivan's class. I never get anything right." He slumped deeper in the chair.

"I think you should have a tutor, someone to help you, one-on-one. Vic was pretty good at math. Maybe he could spare some time. What do you think?" His father waited for an answer.

"I'm trying to work things out on my own," Donavan insisted. "I hate it that everyone is always asking about my math problems. As soon as people see me, the first thing they say is 'Hi, Donnie. How's your math?'" He used a falsetto voice. "It's a math block. No big deal."

His father smiled. "I know how you feel. I hate that kind of attention myself, but I had to learn how to talk about my problems. That's the only way to solve them. What's this about a math block? Talk to me, Donavan." His father looked at Donavan's stubborn expression. "Tell me about your math block."

Donavan took a deep breath and began explaining his troubles. "Dad, we're adding, subtracting, multiplying, and dividing fractions and decimals. I understand in the beginning, but somewhere in the middle of the problem, I get so mixed up and confused. In class I know the answers and I understand the steps. But when I get home and look at my homework, I'm lost."

His father nodded in understanding. "Do you work problems out in class, at the board?"

Donavan winced. "I don't like board work. I really freeze up when I'm in front of the class. I hate everybody staring at me."

"Ummm," his father said.

"See, I write down one answer." Donavan took a paper from the pile and pointed. "It looks right at first, but then I think of something else and change it." He pointed to a scratched-out example. "And then they both look wrong." He sounded miserable.

"Well, you finally got the problem right."

"Yeah, but look at the paper. It's got so many cross-outs, I can't tell what's right and what's wrong." He frowned at the paper. "I spend a lot of time recopying my work."

"Tell me a little bit about your strategy for getting your homework done." His father got up from the desk and reached for a chair.

"Strategy?" Donavan asked. "What's a strategy?"

"Well, a strategy is a careful plan. It's a way to tackle a hard job, get it completed." His father looked at the papers on the table and searched until he found a blank sheet and a pencil. He began to make notes as he spoke. "From the things you've told me, I think that you need to tackle your homework as soon as you come home from school. If you begin as soon as possible, maybe you'll still remember what you did in school that day."

"I always do my math homework last," Donavan said. "Math is my last class and I don't want to think about it right after school. I need a break."

"Maybe you should come home and get out of your school clothes, make yourself comfortable, and then eat a snack. I think you'll feel recharged and ready to tackle your math homework."

Donavan looked at the scattered papers on the table as his father continued. "It makes sense to begin with your math homework while the problems are still fresh in your mind."

Math first thing after school? "I dunno, Dad."

"Got anything better?" his father asked.

"Nope," Donavan admitted. "I guess I could try the strategy tomorrow." He looked doubtful.

"Good deal." His father reached across the table. Donavan smiled and shook his hand.

"Thanks, Dad. I hope I didn't make you too late for Uncle Vic."

His father rose from the chair and looked at his watch. "Don't worry about it. Do you want me to ask your uncle if he has some time to tutor you in math?"

"No, I'm going to try this first." Donavan picked up the paper his father made notes on.

"See you later." His father waved and left the room. Donavan was busy going over his new strategy.

TUESDAY in math class, Donavan made sure he copied his classwork and homework from the board carefully. Pooh and Eric had band practice, so he did not wait around after class.

Donavan raced home, changed his clothes, and fixed

a snack. Then he settled down at his desk. For the first time in a long time, he was ready to do his math homework. He worked on several problems and realized that many weren't too hard to solve. Donavan smiled in surprise. Maybe this strategy would really work!

Ten minutes later he hit a snag and could not understand the next step. He flipped through his notes and then checked his textbooks for examples.

"Oh, snap!" he said in frustration, and scratched his head. Leaning his chair back on two legs, he looked around his room and his aquarium caught his attention.

"Hey, little fishes." Getting up, he walked over to the tank. "You guys hungry?" He reached for the fish food. After he fed the fish, Donavan sat on the floor in front of his bed. Suddenly he remembered a comic book Eric had given him at lunchtime. He dug around in his backpack and found it.

"Man oh man," he said, resting his back against his bed. "I wish I had superpowers." Superheroes probably never had to do math homework. He opened the comic book. Twenty minutes later, he closed the last page.

Donavan stretched and looked down at his feet, noticing that the laces in his sneakers were dirty. Jumping up, he poked around in his desk drawer until he found a fresh pair. He was starting to re-lace his sneakers, when he heard Nikki's voice.

"Donnie, come to dinner!"

Her call surprised him. Looking up at the clock on the wall, he realized that several hours had passed.

At the table his father was carving a roast. "How's your new plan?" he asked, winking.

"What plan?" Nikki demanded.

"Trying something new?" his mom asked.

"Donnie, explain the strategy," his father said proudly.

"Well . . ." Donavan began, telling them all about the ideas he and his dad had discussed. His mother and Nikki asked questions and made suggestions. After dinner Donavan decided to begin again. He forgot several steps and had to check his textbook several times. Each problem took longer than the last.

"Three more," he said wearily. Donavan looked at the clock and realized that his favorite game show began in twenty minutes. He ducked his head and rushed through the remaining problems.

WEDNESDAY in class Mr. Sullivan checked Donavan's homework and shook his head. "You started off great, Donavan, but it looks like you lost energy."

Donavan looked at his paper and realized that he had five correct answers out of ten problems. "Oh, snap!" He decided to take a day off from the strategy and begin again tomorrow. That afternoon he had to stop in the office and check on the wait list for Heritage Month.

"Anybody here?" Donavan looked through the thick

glass pane and tapped on the window. It looked as if the principal's office was empty. "Shucks!" he said, turning away.

The *click, click, click* of heels caught his attention, and he saw Ms. Cassel coming down the hall, walking so fast she almost bumped into Donavan.

"Oops! I just about walked over you." Ms. Cassel dug in her purse and pulled out the office keys. "Sorry, Donavan, I was rushing." Donavan watched as she opened the office door. He followed her inside.

"Donavan," she said, turning on the lights. "I never heard from your grandmother. Is she still interested in the display cases?"

"I don't think so." He remembered the note, the one from Grandma that he'd never given to Ms. Cassel.

"Write your grandmother's telephone number on this paper and I'll call her this evening." Ms. Cassel looked at him. "Donavan, are you listening?"

"Yes," he said, and remembered why he'd kept the note. Uncle Vic was not interested in coming to school and Donavan agreed with him. Ms. Cassel stretched out her hand with the piece of paper in it. He looked at the paper but did not reach for it. "She doesn't need the cases," he said quickly. "They . . . they were for . . . umm, umm . . . they were for my uncle Vic's carved animals." He took a deep breath. "He isn't interested in putting them on display." Donavan looked around the office and shrugged his shoulders. "He said maybe next time."

Ms. Cassel's lips were pressed together and they made a thin line. She tapped one foot on the floor. Donavan had seen this expression before. It meant she was thinking hard about what he had just said. He wondered if she believed it.

"Ummm, well," she said. "Is your uncle coming to any Heritage Month events with your family?"

"I don't think so." He forced himself to look at Ms. Cassel and smile. He wasn't lying to her, he thought. He'd told her the truth. Uncle Vic *wasn't* interested in displaying his carvings and he *didn't* want to come to Heritage Month.

"Okay, Donavan," she said. "Is there anything I can help you with? It looked like you really wanted to get into the office."

"I just wanted to see the wait list." He waited while she went around the desk and found the yellow pad.

"Let me see. Yes, you three guys are still the only ones here."

"Have any more fifth graders signed up?" Donavan held his breath.

"Yes, we have six volunteers." Ms. Cassel laid the pad back on the desk.

"Oh. Thanks."

"See you later." Ms. Cassel walked him to the door. "I'm sorry your uncle changed his mind. It would have been nice to see him again."

"He didn't change his mind," Donavan blurted. "He never wanted to come. My grandma wanted him to." Maybe Ms. Cassel would drop the subject now that she knew Uncle Vic wasn't interested. He hoped so.

On the walk home Donavan thought about the note and wished his grandmother had never written it. He didn't like keeping it, but Grandma should have seen that Uncle Vic didn't want to come to the school. Donavan knew how Vic felt—something like the way Donavan felt when he was up at the board trying to solve a math problem that didn't make any sense. Everybody stared and he felt like a fool. Uncle Vic probably felt the same way. He didn't want to be around people the way he was now. Maybe Grandma didn't know that people stared at Uncle Vic, that they always remembered him as a dancer and a basketball player. "Oh well!" he said glumly. "I did what I thought was right." He thought about what he'd just said, and it didn't make him feel better.

THURSDAY evening Donavan followed his father to the basement, sat on a stool, and watched his dad make labels.

"Hey, buddy, you look like you lost your best friend. What's up?" His father looked at him and then set the label gun on the counter and pushed the pile of colorful labels aside. "Come on, son, let me hear it."

Donavan started from the beginning and explained the failed plan. His father did not interrupt; he just nodded when Donavan made certain points.

"Dad, I don't think the strategy was a good one."

"Ummm. Didn't work for you."

"Nope."

"What did you dislike most about the plan?" his dad asked.

"It was like too much studying. I got tired and wanted to do something else."

His father nodded his head in agreement. "Why don't you try breaking that math homework down into little chunks of time?" He picked up a stout silver can, selected a wide label from the pile and pressed it into place, smoothing it with his thumb. "When I find a job too big, I just break it down into sections."

"How?" Donavan asked, and read the label. "Magenta."

His father scratched his chin. "Before you start your homework, check to see how many problems you have. If you have fifteen, divide them into three sets of five." He glanced at Donavan to make sure he was paying attention. Donavan nodded.

"Get a timer and set it for twenty minutes. That should be enough time to do five problems." He picked up a large green label and applied it to a long white can shaped like a tube. "Take your time and don't rush yourself. If the timer beeps in the middle of a problem, continue until you've finished that one, and then take a break."

"I'm really beginning to like this strategy."

His father continued. "Now, when the timer beeps, you can rest for a little while. Give yourself time to chill out. But don't forget to reset the timer for your break!"

"How long should I rest?" Donavan asked.

"Take no more than ten minutes. Don't leave the room. Do something you really enjoy. With this plan you're doing your homework and you're also rewarding yourself. All right?"

"All right!" Donavan said. He liked the thought of a homework strategy that meant he could take breaks and rest. "Dad, I think it'll work!"

His father chuckled. "Not so fast, son. First you've got to do it."

Donavan nodded. Mr. Sullivan would be so surprised when Donavan handed in his math homework, all complete, all correct!

His father handed Donavan a few labels. "Help me out here, son. I'll write the labels, you can put them on the cans. I'm sorting and labeling these cans of paint. I don't want to forget what's inside."

"Good strategy, Dad." He read the label: "Summer Meadow Green." He began to peel the label. "I'm going to start my new plan Monday."

"Donavan, I like that you're attacking your problem from different angles. But your mom and I are still thinking about a tutor. Your mom thinks a summer math camp would make a difference."

Donavan frowned. Summer school! That didn't sound as good as homework breaks. "Dad, I can get the math when I have a routine. I don't think I'm gonna need to go to school this summer." His father smiled and Donavan continued. "I'm getting more answers right than I used to."

"We'll see." They stuck on several labels before his father said, "Hey, I almost forgot an important part of the strategy." He reached for a plastic apple on the shelf and tossed it to Donavan. "Try this. It's a timer."

CHAPTER 10

HOMEWORK HELPER

All weekend Donavan thought about his plan to overcome his math problems. Monday afternoon on the way home from school, he explained his new strategy to his friends. "What do you guys think? Did I leave anything out?"

"I like it," Eric said. "You got it covered."

Donavan looked past Eric at Pooh. Pooh kept walking. "What you think, Pooh?" Donavan asked, and held his breath; he never knew what Pooh would say.

"Do you still have a math block?" Pooh asked.

"I don't know," Donavan said slowly, trying to figure out what Pooh was thinking. "I'm getting some of my math homework right, but there are always a few kinks. I think I'm better."

"Has anything clicked yet? Are you having a breakthrough?" Pooh looked somber.

"I'm not talking about the block, the click, or the breakthrough," Donavan said impatiently. "What do you think of this plan?"

"Maybe you should call the problems equations," Pooh said thoughtfully.

"Why? What difference would it make?" Eric looked annoyed.

"If you think of them as problems, they'll be problems. If they are equations, they're just something to be solved."

Donavan and Eric's jaws dropped. They slapped Pooh on the back.

"Good point," Donavan said. "But really, Pooh, what do you think about the plan?" No answer. They walked on until Eric could not stand Pooh's silence.

"Say something, Pooh!" he ordered.

"I can't," Pooh said calmly.

"Why not?" both boys asked.

"Because I don't want to jinx the plan."

"How can you jinx his plan?" Eric rolled his eyes.

"It sounds too perfect to me. I can't see anything wrong with it," Pooh said, shaking his head. "If we keep talking about it, we might find something wrong and mess it up."

"Oh!" Donavan said, and smiled.

"Oh yeah, right," Eric agreed.

At home Donavan changed his clothes, made a snack, gathered his books, and looked around his room. *I better take this downstairs,* he thought. *There's too much neat stuff to do in here.*

In the family room he settled at the big table and placed his math book, class notes, and fresh paper in front of him. He was not going to clutter the table with things he did not need. Donavan selected five problems, set the timer, and got to work.

Twenty minutes later, the timer beeped loudly. He looked at his paper and smiled in satisfaction. "This is so cool." He lifted his word jar from a shelf and dumped several slips of paper on the table. He reset the timer for ten minutes and decided to make sure he had written definitions for every word in the jar.

He came across the word *bucktooth* and flipped it over. He laughed at the meaning, grabbed his pencil, and drew two big front teeth sticking from a mouth.

"Man oh man," he said, laughing. "I should have thought of this sooner."

He sorted some more and found the word *gobbledegook.* He looked on the other side, read the definition, and thought for several minutes. Then he drew a cartoon of a little man with a giant megaphone, his scrambled words bursting out of the cone.

The timer beeped, and Donavan pushed the word collection aside and reset the timer. Selecting five new problems, he began working. The problems were not difficult. This time he finished before the timer beeped.

"Great!" he said excitedly, and reached for the pile of words. *I need some more funny words,* he thought. Then he remembered. Uncle Vic had said he was "flabbergasted" at dinner. What did that mean?

He ran for the dictionary, pulled it from the shelf, and began thumbing through the pages until he came to the F's. He read the definition and laughed. The timer beeped loudly. Donavan frowned in confusion and then remembered he finished his second set of problems early. He shut the timer off.

Grabbing a pencil and a blank slip of paper, he wrote *flabbergasted* carefully and then added the definition to the back side of the slip.

Drumming his pencil on the table, he thought and thought until finally he said, "I got it!" First he drew a boy stick figure scratching his head. Next he drew numbers popping out of the boy's head and finally added numbers scattered around the boy's feet. Donavan let out a happy sigh. He totally forgot to reset the timer and worked on his word jar so long that he never got back to his math homework.

* * *

Tuesday afternoon at the end of math class, Mr. Sullivan handed him his homework with the word INCOMPLETE in big red letters across the paper.

"Donavan," he said. "Have one of your parents sign this letter and return it to me." Mr. Sullivan dropped a long, white envelope on the desk. "Oh, and don't forget to have them sign the homework, too." He pointed at the bottom of the homework paper and walked down the aisle.

Donavan moaned and dropped his head on the desk. *The perfect strategy,* he thought, *and I messed it up. It's me. I've got a big, big, math block and nothing can puncture it. I do not get it and I never will. I'm totally flummoxed.* Getting up from the desk, he gathered his things and walked out the door. He looked around for Eric and Pooh and remembered that on Tuesdays they had band practice. He was glad to walk home alone.

At home Donavan didn't change his clothes and he didn't get a snack. He went into the kitchen and sat down. *What am I going to do today?* he thought. *Maybe this time I'll try my plan, but I won't take a break.* No, he didn't want to do that! It seemed like he was back to square one with no plan at all.

Donavan opened his backpack and dumped everything on the table. The long white envelope addressed to his parents sat on top. He looked through the messy papers and saw a square purple envelope. "Oh, snap!" he said, and pulled Grandma's note from the pile. "Big, big trouble. I forgot all about this."

But then he thought, *Not true. Not true at all.* He'd never meant to give Ms. Cassel the note. He didn't want his uncle to come to school and talk about carving or anything else. After Pooh and Eric saw Uncle Vic and they acted just fine around him, Donavan had almost changed his mind. But then a boy at school, Curtis Simmons, stopped Donavan in the lunchroom and asked, "Does your uncle know what they did with his legs?" Donavan had looked at him to see if he was joking. But Curtis looked serious. "No" was all Donavan had answered before he walked away.

He knew Curtis wouldn't be the only person to ask stupid questions. There would probably be many more.

Donavan tucked Grandma's note back in his pack and picked up his homework paper from Monday. He looked at the scribbled problems and the many spots where he'd erased and crossed out wrong answers. The paper was a mess. He hadn't noticed how it looked when he turned it in.

"I can't stand this!" Donavan crunched the paper up and threw it at the tall trash can in the corner. "Slam dunk!" he said as the ball of paper disappeared into the can. "Math, stop messing with me!"

"Who you talking to?" Nikki asked, peeping into the room.

"Math," Donavan said, and took a clean sheet of paper from his notebook.

"Oh, I like math." Nikki took a chair next to him. He watched as she leaned over and looked at his notebook. "What type of math you doing?"

"Multiplication. And you don't know a thing about it," he said, and began his homework.

"Grumpy Gus." Nikki leaned closer to look at the assignment. "Maybe I can help you. I know my multiplication tables backwards and forwards from one to twelve. I don't have to look at the answers."

"So?" Donavan said, raising his arm to block Nikki's view.

"So let me look at it." Nikki reached for the paper.

Donavan could tell from the expression on her face that she would not leave until he let her see the problem. "You're two whole grades behind me. How are you going to figure this problem out?" he demanded.

"'Cause I'm good. Everybody says so. I go to a higher grade for math." She moved closer to the paper.

"Your class isn't doing this type of problem." Moving the paper away from her, he leaned back in the chair. "I was in Ms. Paylor's class. I didn't have this type of multiplication problem until I got to Mr.

Sullivan's class this year."

"Let me see." Nikki insisted. "I love numbers and numbers love me."

"That's crazy. How can numbers love you?" Donavan rolled his eyes.

"I know they love me because they come to me when I think of them." She reached for the textbook.

"This is silly." Donavan put his pencil on the paper and slid it in front of her. His smile was smug. "All right, little Miss Einstein, go for it. Let me see what you can do."

He picked up his map and began to work on his geography homework. He loved geography, especially maps. Discovering interesting towns and countries with strange names was fun. When Uncle Vic went to boot camp, Donavan's mother bought a map and hung it on the wall in the family room. Donavan found Fort Jackson, South Carolina. Later, when Uncle Vic was stationed at bases in other countries, he'd mark those places on the map.

In his letters to his uncle, Donavan wanted to know everything about wherever he was. How did the people dress? What did they eat? How did their language sound? In those days Uncle Vic's letters were filled with exciting stories; but now that he was home, those countries were never mentioned. Donavan wondered if it would be all right to ask him about the place where his tragedy happened. He sighed, put down the map, and looked over at Nikki.

She was chewing on the pencil's eraser and moving her lips slowly, but she didn't make a sound. He decided to give her a few more minutes and then he would take his paper back and finish the problems.

"Look at this," Nikki said, and slid the paper in front of Donavan. "I think it's almost right."

Donavan looked at the paper and checked the answer. He checked twice before he looked at Nikki. "I think this is right," he said in wonder. "I don't know how you got it, but I think it is."

"I just kept multiplying and adding the leftover numbers to the next column," she said in a matter-of-fact way. "Let me show you." Nikki moved closer to Donavan and used the pencil as a pointer as she talked him through the problem.

"You see?" she asked. "I think you keep forgetting to carry the leftover numbers to the next digit."

"Yeah, but . . ." That was all Donavan could bring himself to say. He chewed on his bottom lip. "Dag, Nikki, I know you love numbers but . . ." He stopped talking and rechecked the answer. "You're two grades behind me and you solved the problem."

"It didn't feel like a problem." She grinned.

"Have you multiplied three place numbers before?" he asked.

"Yes, in a math workbook Uncle Vic gave me. He told me to work on the ones I could by myself and he would show me the rest." She wore a proud grin.

"Why are you doing problems that your class isn't working on?" He could not understand anyone wanting to do extra math. "That's weird!"

"It's not weird—it's fun." Nikki giggled. "I do them because I want to and I like figuring numbers out. I told you, they aren't problems to me." She thought for a moment. "You like filling jars with words. You look for new words all the time. I like numbers the same way." Nikki stood up. "Call me if you need help," she said breezily, and walked over to the cookie jar.

"Yeah, right!" Donavan mumbled.

Nikki left the kitchen singing through a mouthful of cookie.

CHAPTER 11

HAPPY WORD WORK

"Hey, Grandma, T.G.I.T." Donavan looked at the snacks on the table and tried to decide which ones he wanted. He decided the chips looked best. He scooped a handful into a napkin and began to munch.

"I thought it was T.G.I.F." Grandma set a tray with a pitcher and two glasses on the table.

"I changed Friday to Thursday. I'm glad the week is almost over." Donavan picked one of the glasses from the tray. "Mmm, lemonade."

"It's freshly squeezed. I see you have everything ready." She checked. "Board, dictionary, tile racks, pencils, timer, and

score pad." Grandma sat across from him in her armchair. "Did you have a hard week?"

"The worst! I couldn't wait for Thursday. I need some fun."

"Fun, fun." Grandma laughed. "Sounds like you expect to win this week."

"I'm feeling real lucky today." Donavan grabbed a handful of pretzels from a bowl. "Get ready," he warned, wiped his hand on his napkin, and studied the letters on his tile rack. Every Thursday after school he visited his Grandma at her apartment, and they always began the afternoon playing a game of Scrabble.

Donavan put down the first word of the game: *ABACUS.* He counted his points. "Eleven points, a double word, that's twenty-two points. I'm starting strong." Donavan selected six new tiles and waited. "Your turn."

"I know," Grandma said, looking at the board. Grandma almost always won, but today Donavan thought that just might change. Didn't he deserve some good luck after all the time he'd spent trying to fix his math block?

"Gee whiz. That's a math word, isn't it?" she asked.

"Yup! Mr. Ang has an abacus. It's been in his family for years." He watched Grandma spell the word *MIST* around the *S* in *ABACUS.* "You got two double letters,

Grandma. Your score is eight."

Donavan placed a *Y* under the *M* in *MIST.* "I'm hot! The Y is a triple letter. That makes fifteen. My new score is thirty-seven. Hot! Hot! Hot!" He cackled gleefully.

"My oh my," Grandma said. "You don't seem to have math trouble adding up our scores."

"That's because it's not decimals or fractions, just adding and subtracting." He selected another tile and studied his letters. Being with Grandma on their Thursday always cheered him up. Their routine was to play Scrabble, talk about anything and everything, and then eat dinner. After dinner they'd go down to the lobby to wait for one of his parents to pick him up. While waiting he'd visit her friends and neighbors. It was fun to listen to their old-timey talk. The seniors loved to tell him how the world was when they were young.

"Donavan," Mr. Bill Gut had said in his gravelly voice last week, "television didn't exist when I was your age. We'd sit around and listen to the radio." Donavan's expression was doubtful.

"Sit around and listen to a radio?"

"Yup, we'd listen to plays. We really used our imagination back then."

Mr. Foote quickly joined the conversation. "Some of those radio plays were very, very scary. After I listened,

I'd be so frightened I wouldn't close my eyes." The seniors in the lobby had laughed and agreed.

Now, after looking at the board several minutes, Grandma clapped her hands in delight. "Oh my goodness! I got a good word. *O-P-T-I,* she spelled, laying each of the tiles in front of the word *MIST*. "Optimist," she said grandly. "Count 'em up."

Counting quickly, Donavan added seventeen points to her score. "Twenty-five," he said. While Grandma added four new letters to her tile rack, Donavan reached for the paperback dictionary on the table beside the board.

"Optimist: someone who takes a hopeful and positive view of future outcomes. Cool. I'd like to be an optimist, especially with math." He set the dictionary on the table.

"Why was this week so stressful?" Grandma asked.

"Grandma, Nikki solved one of my math problems," he complained. "It's bad enough that I'm having trouble, but then Nikki walked in and solved the whole thing." He snapped his fingers. "Just like that. I wanted to scream. It's the pits." He shook his head in disbelief. "My little sister did my math homework."

"Goodness, now, that sounds pretty stressful."

Donavan looked at his grandmother to see if she was teasing him. She didn't look as if she was. "If my friends ever found out, they'd tease me forever," he said.

"I can see why that would upset you. But Donnie, I've seen you help Nikki with her spelling homework many times." Grandma waited for Donavan's response.

"I know, but I'm her big brother. I'm supposed to help her out." He looked down at his letters and gave her a sly grin.

"What you got?" Grandma asked, leaning forward.

"Time." He laid *I-M-E* under the last *T* in *OPTIMIST*.

Grandma watched Donavan tally the score. "How much?" she asked.

"Forty-three."

"Boy oh boy! You're doing well today. I have to keep my wits sharp. How do you always find just the right word?" Grandma smiled in admiration.

"I guess I'm lucky and I like playing with words. I just wish I was lucky with numbers too."

"You may be lucky, but you're always thinking about words, looking for words, and collecting words. I don't think it's just luck. It's also hard work."

"Grandma, why does everyone think that I don't work hard enough at math? I do. I don't like math because I've always had a hard time." He slumped back on the sofa.

"I didn't mean that you don't work hard. I know you do. You're a very optimistic person. I see you trying one thing and then another. You never give up. I like that about you." She picked up the pitcher of lemonade and refilled his glass.

"I try," Donavan said with a sigh. He wished he could stop trying for once and just succeed.

"Would it be such a bad idea if Nikki helped you out once in a while?"

"I dunno."

"You're certainly an excellent big brother, always ready to help your little sister." Grandma winked. "Maybe she could repay you."

Her words surprised Donavan. After a few moments of silence he said, "You know, Grandma? You're right. Nikki owes me big-time. Yeah, I might let her help me."

He saw Grandma look at the board and smile. He knew that smile. She'd found a new word. He sat up, and, sure enough, she placed the word *QUIBBLE* on the board, using the *B* in *ABACUS*.

"That's awesome!" He opened the dictionary and read the definition aloud. "To argue over unimportant things." He raised an eyebrow and looked at his grandmother sternly. "Grandma, are you saying I was quibbling over Nikki helping me with my homework?" He tried to look serious, but a chuckle escaped.

"No, no, no. I think your problems are real, Donnie, but I'm optimistic that you'll overcome them." She laughed quietly. "Count my score. I think my luck just changed."

"Wow, that one word is eighty points!" His eyes widened. "The word is twenty points, then doubled to forty and then doubled again. Unbelievable." Donavan leaned closer and recounted the points. "Yup! It's eighty points. Total score: one hundred and five."

"Yes indeed! I'm in the lead," Grandma said, and reached for six more tiles.

"Nikki is good with numbers," Donavan said, pleased. "She's good in science, too. I'm proud of her. It's just that I was surprised."

"One is good with words; the other is good with numbers. I'm glad that you have each other. Y'all make a good team." Grandma looked at her tile rack and made a face. "Oh, I forgot to ask. Did Ms. Cassel ever say anything about the note that I sent her?"

"The note?" Donavan asked absently. He was trying to find a new word.

"Yes, the note I sent to Ms. Cassel. It's been a while."

"Oh, yeah, the note." Donavan shifted in his seat. "She, she, umm, she said she was pretty busy."

"I understand. I just thought that she would have answered by now. It's been several weeks."

"I think she said she was going to check with Ms. Strickland to see if there was any more space in the display cases." He thought, *I should tell Grandma I didn't give Ms. Cassel the note.*

Grandma looked at the board carefully. "I'll wait and give her a few more days."

Donavan quickly thought of a solution. He would give Ms. Cassel the note tomorrow and tell her he'd forgotten it. He felt better. It was probably too late anyway; the display cases would be full. Uncle Vic was safe. No one would stare at him and ask a lot of dumb questions. He looked at the board again and saw a new word.

"H," Donavan said, placing the letter in front of the *E* in the word *TIME.* "R-O. Hero. Eleven points for the word. I'm up to Fifty-four."

Grandma swiftly used the *O* in *HERO* to create *OWL.*

"That's six. You're up to one hundred eleven." Looking over the board carefully, Donavan used the *L* in *OWL* to create the word *LOVE.*

"Good. Fourteen points. I'm catching up with you, Grandma."

"Ummm. Donnie, I think I'll call Ms. Cassel tomorrow. I'd love to see Vic's animal collection on display during Heritage Month."

Donavan thought of how his uncle had acted during the welcome-home dinner. "Grandma, Uncle Vic didn't seem like he cared about the display." He glanced at her to see her reaction. Grandma seemed to be concentrating on the board. "He was so quiet. He only answered questions."

"Yes," she said sadly. "I noticed that. I hope that participating in Heritage Month might cheer him up."

Donavan hesitated before saying, "Maybe he doesn't want to go around people. It might be hard to be different."

"I'm sure it is." Grandma's reply was quiet.

"He can't do any of the things he used to do. I'll bet he wishes every day that he wasn't in a wheelchair. I hate seeing him in that chair!" Donavan blinked in surprise. He had not meant to say that. Would his grandmother mind? Would she be angry? But she was only quiet, so he continued.

"It makes me feel bad to see him, and then I feel bad because I feel bad. Is it wrong to feel sorry that Uncle Vic will never be like he used to be?"

"No, it's not wrong. You love your uncle and you want things to be the way they were. The only thing that will help is time. It takes time to get used to change."

He kept his eyes down, looking at the board. "Do you feel mad about what happened, Grandma?"

"Yes. I think I got the perfect word. "P-I-"—she used the *Q* in *QUIBBLE*—"U-E. This is how I felt on lots of days. Pique."

"Pique. That sounds funny. What's it mean?"

"Pique means a bad mood or a feeling of resentment.

That's how I felt for a long time. Then I began to accept what happened to Vic. I'm better now, but there are still times when I feel angry."

"Oh," Donavan said, surprised. "Do you think Uncle Vic is piqued?"

"Yes," she replied.

Because he didn't know what to say, Donavan said nothing. He began tallying the score. "Grandma, you're leaving me in the dust. Sixteen points for *pique* and your total is one hundred twenty-seven. But I'm still going to catch up."

Donavan placed a blank tile above the *E* in *LOVE* and put *H* above the blank tile.

"What's the word?" Grandma asked.

"H-U-E. Want to know what it means?" He didn't wait for an answer. "Hue, a specific shade of a particular color." His smile was smug.

"What color?" Grandma asked.

"Every color has a hue. Lots of hues."

"You don't get any points for that blank tile," she reminded him.

"I know."

Grandma's next word, *DESK*, gained nine points. Donavan created *DEW* using the *D* in *DESK*. Grandma quickly used the *K* in *DESK* to spell *KEG*.

"What's the score?" she asked.

Donavan read from the pad. "Grandma: one hundred forty-six." He paused.

"Grandson: eighty-seven. Dag." Donavan frowned. "My granny is whipping me."

"Sounds good to me," Grandma said, looking at her tiles.

"Ummm." Donavan concentrated on the board. He rearranged the tiles on his tray and frowned.

"Donnie, you've got a lot going on in your life," Grandma said. "I know you're busy trying to get better grades in math. And your uncle's accident is still a problem."

Donavan scratched his head. "Sometimes, Grandma, I feel like a Ping-Pong ball. I just bounce from math to Uncle Vic." He wagged his head from side to side.

Grandma laughed and Donavan did too.

"Donnie, that's funny. Well, I want you to remember that both of your problems can be solved with patience and some sharp thinking. You keep working on them; you'll get a breakthrough."

"I hope so. Grandma, did you forget dinner?"

"No. But I've been winning at this game, and I forgot to heat the food." She got up from her chair.

"What are we having?" He rearranged his tiles again.

"Jambalaya."

"Ummm. Did you fix dirty rice or yellow rice?"

“Saffron rice, a cucumber salad, and ambrosia for dessert.” She winked. “How’s that?”

“Good, good, good.” He focused on the board. “I wish I had the letters for jambalaya,” he said wistfully.

“Humph! I don’t see that happening.” Grandma looked down at the board. “No, I don’t see that at all.”

“I think I’m going to trade in five of my letters.” Donavan chewed his lower lip.

“That’s a turn,” Grandma reminded him.

“I know.” Donavan turned five of his tiles over and selected five that were lying facedown next to the board. He slid his old tiles into the pile and shuffled them around. “Okay, I’m ready for a new start.”

“Oh, I see something.” Grandma leaned over and put an *O* over the *W* in *DEW* and a *T* over the *O*. “Tow. That’s six points and a double word. Twelve points.”

Donavan reached for the pencil and added twelve to Grandma’s one hundred forty-six. “New score is one hundred fifty-eight.”

“Now I’m going to heat our dinner.” She straightened up. “Don’t touch that board!”

Donavan laughed. “Grandma, I don’t cheat. I win!”

“Game ain’t over yet,” Grandma called.

“Wait a minute, Miz Grandma. I think it is!” Grandma stopped in the doorway to the kitchen and watched as Donavan stood up and waved his hands in the air.

"Bam!" He started at the top of the board and said each letter out loud as he laid it down. "F-A-N-D-A-N-G." Then the letter *O* from the word *OPTIMIST* was there. "O!" he exclaimed in triumph. "Fifty extra points! Seven tiles at once gets fifty extra points. Hey, Grandma, this is my fandango dance. Come on!" He grabbed her hand and they both danced around the table.

"My goodness! Boy, you're wearing me out. I'm going to fix our dinner." Grandma danced into the kitchen.

"Hey, Grandma, loser does the dishes," Donavan called. "I guess this optimistic stuff really works!" He sat down and added his points. "Fandango is twelve points, one triple letter makes it fifteen, and a double word makes it thirty. That adds to one hundred seventeen. And, when I add my fifty extra points, I have a grand total of one hundred sixty-seven." He grinned wide enough to hurt. "Donavan: one hundred sixty-seven. Miz Grandma: one hundred fifty-eight minus thirteen points from leftover tiles. Her not-so-grand total is one hundred forty-five points."

Donavan laughed. "Hey, Grandma, are you piqued?"

CHAPTER 12

HAVING A BAD DAY

"What a stupid Saturday morning!" Donavan raised his window shade and looked out. The thick clouds made everything gray and foggy. He noticed that the tree in the backyard was dancing in the wind, its bare branches sweeping the ground.

March is coming in like a lion, he thought, and turned from the window to get dressed.

An hour later Donavan entered the kitchen. "Morning," he said to his mom, and sat in a chair at the table. "Where's Nikki?"

His mom placed a bowl of oatmeal in front of him. "She's with your father. They went to pick up some supplies for Heritage Month." She put a pitcher of milk in front of him. "Eat up."

Donavan reached for the shaker of brown sugar. He sprinkled some over his oatmeal until his mother gave him a look that said "enough." He tasted a spoonful and licked his lips.

"Umm, just like I like it." He ate in silence, remembering his big win at Scrabble and how he'd picked up several super words for his collection. Thinking about the word *optimist*, he was ready to plan a new strategy for conquering his math block.

"Can you believe Heritage Month is just a month away?" his mother asked, sitting next to him. "I promised to help Miz Utz in the office. I don't know where I'll find the time."

Donavan instantly recalled the note in his backpack. He hadn't had time on Friday to take it to Ms. Cassel. Suddenly the oatmeal tasted gluey and bitter.

"What are your plans for today?" His mom was writing on a notepad.

"Studying a little," he said, and pushed his bowl aside.

"Will you do me a favor?" His mother got up. "I'll be right back."

Donavan stared at his bowl. He knew he was going to have to do something about that note, but what, he didn't know. *Big trouble is on the way,* he thought glumly.

"Donavan, I need you to take this package to Vic. Your uncle Gilbert wanted him to have these old carving tools." She set the package on the table. "Do you mind?"

"No," Donavan said quietly. "I'll go now." He picked up the package and headed for the hall closet. Maybe he would think of something on the way over to Uncle Vic's.

Donavan opened the gate to Uncle Vic's yard slowly and waited to hear the dogs barking. "Hey, Mutt. Hey, Jeff," he called. Looking around for the missing dogs, he noticed that the garage door was half-raised. *Maybe Uncle Vic is inside and can't hear me*, he thought.

Donavan bent over and peered inside the garage. In the dim light he saw a mountain of objects, stacked high and wide. He blinked, trying to make his eyes adjust. Laying his package on the ground, he ducked under the door and entered. He noticed a rattan chair sitting atop several crates; the seat was broken and tattered.

No wonder Uncle Vic's workroom is so neat. Everything's in here! He backed into a large wooden statue of a bird. "Oops!" Turning quickly, he grabbed the bird to keep it from toppling. Carefully backing away from the bird, he nearly fell when his foot skidded across the floor. Looking down, he saw a rusty red toy truck under his foot and bent down to pick it up. It was not a toy, he realized, but a model of an old fire engine. Its ladder dangled from the back like a broken arm. He was careful when he set it on an old leather trunk. *This place is so cool. It's like an old junkyard.* He wandered farther inside the garage.

"Whoa!" He flinched when something brushed against his shoulder. "What the . . ." It was the foot of a skeleton hanging from the rafters, glowing in the dim light. He reached up, jiggled the foot, and chuckled when the plastic skeleton began to dance. Just then he heard the sound of barking dogs.

Donavan cocked his head, trying to hear more clearly. The barking stopped for a few seconds and then started again. This time the sound was frantic. Pushing the skeleton aside, he ran from the garage toward the house.

"Oh my gosh!" Donavan ran to the basement door and bumped hard against it. It was locked. Turning quickly, he ran up a ramp to the kitchen door. "Please be open," he panted, and grabbed the knob. It twisted easily under his hand, and the door swung in. No one was there.

Donavan looked around. Before he could call his

uncle's name, the wild barking began again. This time the sound was nearer.

"Mutt! Jeff! I'm coming!" Taking a gulp of air, Donavan ran through the kitchen toward the hall. Turning the corner, Donavan headed for the stairs.

"Ahhhh!" Donavan yelled as Mutt and Jeff jumped against him from behind. He nearly fell. "What? What? What?" he asked, grabbing the stair rail. "Stop it!" He tried to climb the stairs and Jeff shoved against his knees. "What?" he asked again, and realized that the dogs did not want him to go upstairs. When he tried to move around them, Mutt pushed Donavan off the steps.

"Mutt, Jeff, where's Uncle Vic?" Donavan realized that he was almost screaming and tried to calm himself. He needed to think. The dogs whined and pawed at him before they ran down the hallway behind the stairs. Donavan followed.

"Uncle Vic! Uncle Vic!" His voice sounded as anxious as the dog's barking. Donavan followed the dogs through the bedroom door. "Uncle Vic!" He saw his uncle lying on the floor, facedown. His stomach flip-flopped and his legs shook like Jell-O.

Donavan moved closer, blinking several times, trying to understand what he was seeing. Uncle Vic was wearing a long-sleeved T-shirt and pair of shorts, and it looked like he had legs. Legs?

"Huh?" Donavan said loudly as his knees buckled and he sat down heavily. Hesitantly, he reached out to touch Uncle Vic's shoulder.

"Uncle Vic?" he pleaded, nudging him. "Are you all right? Can you hear me?"

"Donnie?" Uncle Vic's voice was hoarse. "Champ?"

"It's me, Donnie. Uncle Vic?" Donavan tried to keep his voice low and steady as he slid his hands under Uncle Vic's shoulder and tried to lift. "Can you turn over?"

"Donnie, you have to move my legs." Uncle Vic croaked. "They're twisted up."

"Legs?" Donavan's brain refused to understand. "Your legs?" he asked again and looked down. Leather, metal, and a shoe, he thought. It made no sense.

The dogs crowded each other, trying to lick Uncle Vic. "Stop, boys! Move!" Donavan gave the dogs a push. They backed up a little, but they would not leave Vic's side.

Donavan's gaze traveled down his uncle's back, past his shorts to his thighs and his knees. Under the shorts it looked as if his legs were wrapped in white socks. Each calf disappeared into a thick brown leather cup.

Donavan reached out to touch one of the cups and then jerked back. "Um, um, um," he said, trying to push

words out of his throat. But they kept sliding back down. He expelled a deep breath and pushed his question out. "I—I don't know what to do."

"My legs. They got twisted." His uncle coughed to clear his throat. "Begin at the foot, near the ankle, the hinge. I think the legs are crossed there. You'll need to lift the right leg."

"Can you turn over?" Slipping his hands under Uncle Vic's shoulder, he pushed again.

"No, Champ. Uncross the legs first."

Donavan looked away from his uncle and glanced anxiously around the room. *There is no one but me,* he thought. *I've got to do it.* Donavan took a deep breath and scooted down to the sneaker at the end of one metal leg. He could not decide what to touch first, so he looked closely at it, trying to figure what was what.

Attached to the leather cup that held the calf was a long, smooth tubelike metal rod. On a hinge at the end of the rod was the sneaker. Donavan could see that the tangle was at the hinged part. He wiped the sweat from his forehead on the sleeve of his jacket and leaned closer.

Okay, he thought. *The hinge is like an ankle.* And it had caught on the sneaker of the left foot. "I think I understand," Donavan said, and tugged at the right sneaker. He pulled gently and then stopped. "Did that hurt?" he asked timidly.

"No, I can't feel that," Uncle Vic said. "Yank it."

"Will I break it?" Uncle Vic shook his head. Donavan pulled on the foot with more force. Bending closer, he yanked the sneaker. "Oh!" he gasped, dropping the leg, when the shoe came loose from the foot. He held the shoe for a second and then dropped it as if it burned his hand. Looking down, he saw that the legs were no longer touching. "It's done," he said, sitting back on his heels and wiping his sweaty hands on his pant leg.

"Ahhh." Uncle Vic's sigh of relief was good to hear.

Donavan crawled up to his uncle's head, put his arms under his shoulders, and pushed.

"Uumph!" Uncle Vic rolled over on his back. "My, my, my," he said. But rolling over had made Uncle Vic's legs cross again. Donavan crawled back down and rearranged them so that they were in the right position. Uncle and nephew breathed in and out, and the harsh sounds filled the room. The dogs stood quietly, watching them. Uncle Vic grabbed the bottom of his T-shirt and used it to wipe the sweat from his face. Donavan looked down at the splayed legs; the sneaker on the right shoe was still on.

"Get my chair and bring it over here." Uncle Vic's raspy voice startled Donavan.

Donavan looked around and saw the wheelchair sitting by the desk. He scrambled to his feet and grabbed it. Rolling it over to where his uncle lay, he watched closely as Uncle Vic pushed himself up using his elbows until he was in a sitting position. Donavan held the chair steady while his uncle propped himself against it and rested.

"I'm all right, just a little winded," he said, exhaling; he smiled when Mutt and Jeff came to him and started to lick his face. "I'm fine, boys. Down!" He gave them a shove. "Out!" he said, pointing to the door. The dogs circled each other and then settled themselves at the bedroom door.

"Oh boy!" Uncle Vic began to tug at the cup that kept one of the legs attached to his body. "Getting used to these legs is taking more effort than I realized. Twist and pull that leg," he said, pointing to the left one.

Donavan reached out and then stopped. He looked at the leg.

"Donnie, twist the leg. It won't hurt me." Uncle Vic's voice was firm.

Donavan kneeled and grasped the metal leg firmly. He began to turn and pull the thick, brown leather cup attached to his uncle's calf. After a few efforts, he stopped, unbuttoned his jacket, slipped it off, and wiped his face on the sleeve of his shirt.

Okay, okay, I can do this, he told himself. He lifted the leg again and pulled. Donavan heard a pop that sounded like the seal of a can opening.

"Done!" he said, relieved, when he saw Uncle Vic pull what was left of his leg from the leather cup. Donavan blinked. He'd never thought about what Uncle Vic's legs looked like now. The leg ended just below the knee. Without thinking, he pushed the leather and metal leg aside and reached out to touch his uncle's thigh. The flesh under the thin stocking was warm and firm.

"Undo the other leg," Uncle Vic instructed. He watched while his nephew, more confident now, pulled on the right artificial leg and popped it free. "That's a relief." Uncle Vic rubbed his thigh. "Feels good."

Donavan watched while Vic began to massage first

one leg and then the other. "Did you hurt your legs?" he asked quietly.

Uncle Vic shook his head. "No, but I'm glad you stopped by, nephew. I was in here practicing and I got tangled up. Don't ask me how." Uncle Vic's smile looked uneasy, but he seemed okay. "Hold my chair," he said. Donavan stood and held the chair steady. He reached down to take Uncle Vic's arm. But when Uncle Vic shook his head, refusing help, Donavan stood back.

"I've got it," Uncle Vic said sharply, and then smiled to soften his words. "Did I scare you?" He swung up into the chair and settled himself. "I think I scared myself a bit." He wheeled his chair easily over to the desk.

Donavan followed him and sat in the chair beside the desk. He closed his eyes and leaned back. Pulling his shirt from his jeans, he mopped his forehead and then his face. He tried to think of something to say, something funny, but his mind was still stuck on finding Uncle Vic in a tangle on the floor.

"Can you do me a favor?" Uncle Vic asked. Donavan opened his eyes and bobbed his head up and down. "Don't mention this little incident to anyone. I don't want everyone fussing over me."

Donavan bit his bottom lip and listened.

"I just want to be left alone for a while. I seem to make everyone nervous." He laid both hands, palms down, on the desktop.

"Do you mean the family?" Donavan asked, puzzled. He thought everyone was trying to make Uncle Vic feel welcome.

"I feel like the family is trying to rush me back into the world. It's like they're saying, 'Vic, you've fallen, and now all you have to do is get back up.'" Uncle Vic stopped talking and looked down at his hands. "It ain't that easy. I didn't just fall down. I lost my way of being Vic Carter Johnson."

Donavan wasn't sure what he should say. Would there be anything that would make it better? "Is there someone you could ask?" he said hesitantly. "Maybe someone who got lost too?" He hoped that that didn't sound stupid.

Uncle Vic chuckled. "Champ, when you're grown up, I guess there are some things you got to figure out by yourself."

Donavan didn't know if his uncle would like his next question, but he had to ask. "Is it safe for you to be walking on your new legs by yourself?"

"Safe?" Uncle Vic smiled sadly "I thought it was. I began practicing walking with my legs at the rehab center. I've had them for quite a while. I used to go to physical therapy class, but I got frustrated and stopped. I stopped using the legs at all."

"You quit?" Donavan asked in surprise.

"Yes, I guess I did quit." Uncle Vic's voice sounded tired. "I was having so much trouble. It seemed easier to use the wheelchair." He shrugged his shoulders. "I don't know if I'm ever going to get the hang of these legs."

"Shouldn't you keep trying?" Donavan thought for a moment. "My father says that people have to do hard things. He thinks that's the only way they get better."

"Uh-huh," Uncle Vic grunted softly.

"He says that the things we fear look bigger if we don't tackle them. That's what he told me about my math block. Maybe you need a strategy, a plan to get yourself back on your feet."

Donavan saw Uncle Vic's lips form into a smile. He realized what he'd just said. "I didn't mean that to be funny. I just meant you've got to get up and running." Donavan clamped his hands over his mouth.

"Man oh man," Uncle Vic said, still smiling. "You're beginning to sound like your friend Pooh!"

"Oh no!" Donavan said.

"How is your math doing, Champ?" Uncle Vic wheeled his chair closer to Donavan. "Your dad's told me how much trouble you're having."

Donavan leaned over and propped his elbows on his knees. "Sometimes I think I'm getting better. But I just can't seem to keep on track. I guess I've got to keep trying until I get there."

Uncle Vic cocked his head and listened. Donavan kept talking.

"Grandma says I've got to stay optimistic. It's hard, but I'm working on it."

"Ummm," Uncle Vic said, listening.

Donavan remembered the package. "Uncle Vic, I almost forgot why I came!" He explained about the tools.

"Your uncle Gilbert just won't quit." Uncle Vic raised an eyebrow. "Where is the package?"

"I forgot it when I heard the dogs barking. I'll go get it." Donavan stood up and headed for the door, but stopped when he thought of something. "Uncle Vic, do you want to do a program about your carvings?" When he saw the puzzled expression on his uncle's face, he explained. "During Heritage Month, at our school? Do you want to come and talk about your carvings?" That was the simple question. After all, they were Uncle Vic's carvings. All Donavan had ever needed to do was just to ask him what he wanted.

"No, I don't," Vic replied. "Or I didn't when it first came up. Momma wants me to. I didn't think I was ready to visit a school. But you know how it is when your grandmother gets a good idea."

"Can't you tell her you're not ready?" Donavan walked over to Uncle Vic's chair. "Grandma usually understands everything."

"Well, I was trying to get ready. That's why I decided to practice walking with my legs. I wanted to walk into that school." Uncle Vic scratched his head. "But I guess I'll have to find a new plan." His voice sounded tired.

Donavan did not have an answer. "I'm going to find where I dropped your package, Uncle Vic. I'll be right back." He turned and ran from the room.

LATER THE SAME DAY

"I guess I'll have to wash the dishes," Donavan said, wiping his mouth on his napkin. "Uncle Vic, you make good tacos."

Uncle Vic patted his stomach. "I don't want to make them too good or I'll put on weight."

"You look much better now. When I saw you in the hospital, you were too skinny." Donavan picked his dishes up and headed for the sink.

"Yeah, I was." Uncle Vic began to stack the used dishes on the table in a pile. "Did you call your mom and tell her you were staying?" he asked.

"She said I could spend the night." Donavan poured

dishwashing liquid in the pan and turned on both faucets. "If you didn't mind."

After he'd found the package on the garage floor, he'd gone back into the house and asked Uncle Vic if he could stay and visit. He worried about leaving Uncle Vic alone, even though he said he was fine.

"Hey, Uncle Vic," Donavan said looking over his shoulder. "Do you wanna play some Spades after I finish?"

"Spades?" Uncle Vic bunched his face up. "Gosh, you still remember how to play?"

"I'm better than I was the last time we played," Donavan boasted. "I almost always beat Pooh and Eric."

"Okay, we'll see if that happens with me." Uncle Vic pushed the stacked dishes to the end of the table. "Donavan, I used to be pretty good in math. Maybe we could do a few problems and go over your new plan."

Donavan picked up a pile of plates and set them in the sudsy water. *We're having such a good time,* he thought. *I don't want to ruin things*. And math always ruined things. "Today?" he asked reluctantly.

Uncle Vic chuckled. "Yeah, today. After I beat you at a few games of Spades, we'll go over your plan. No time like the present."

"All right." Donavan suddenly had an idea. "Uncle

Vic, I'm getting good with making strategies. Why don't I help you to make a plan?"

"Why do I need a plan?" His uncle sounded suspicious.

"You need a plan to start practicing walking on your legs." Donavan did not turn around from washing the dishes. "No time like the present."

1.86
x1.25
93

CHAPTER 13

HARD WORK

Donavan looked down at the dining-room table and smiled, satisfied that he was ready to begin his new homework plan. He had cleared away everything except his pens, pencils, math textbook, and notebook. His backpack lay on the floor next to the table. He remembered Uncle Vic's main advice: "No distractions."

The two of them had worked on the plan most of Saturday and Sunday afternoon, and later Sunday evening Uncle Vic had tutored him on basic multiplication, single, double, and triple digits. After his tutoring, they ate, traded family news, and played cards.

Donavan asked his uncle several times about making a schedule to practice with his legs, but Uncle Vic had always come up with a way not to talk about it.

Now the weekend was over. It was Monday afternoon, and he was ready to begin working on his latest math strategy. Uncle Vic suggested they call it "the blended plan." Donavan had used parts of every strategy he'd tried so far.

"Working hard?" Nikki asked, walking into the dining room.

"I'm getting ready to start my homework." Donavan looked at the table again to see if he had missed anything. "I was with Uncle Vic this weekend, and he helped me with my new blended plan and some multiplication problems."

"I thought you didn't want to be around Uncle Vic," Nikki said, sitting in a chair.

"Nikki!" Donavan was surprised. "I never, ever said that!"

"You didn't say it; you acted like it." She folded her arms across her chest.

"Yeah, I did," he admitted quietly. "But I'm getting better and I'm getting used to the way Uncle Vic is now."

"Good. Because he's the same Uncle Vic. Only his legs are missing."

"He's not just the same, Nikki. He's changed," Donavan argued.

Nikki nodded. "Sometimes I feel sad for Uncle Vic."

She looked at Donnie, expecting him to reply. When he didn't, she continued. "Is Uncle Vic sad?"

Donavan thought about his conversation with Uncle Vic when he found him on the floor. He remembered his promise not to tell anyone. He twisted his mouth to one side, trying to decide what he could say.

"Sometimes I guess he's a little sad. But he's getting better." Donavan smiled to make Nikki believe him.

She looked closely at Donavan and then said, "Okay." Nikki unfolded her arms and looked at the paper fastened to Donavan's notebook. "What's this?" she asked.

Donavan removed the paper clip and lifted the paper. "This is my checklist after I finish doing my homework."

"When you getting started?" Nikki asked.

"As soon as you leave."

"You might need me," Nikki reminded him with a wide grin.

"I might. You helped me before and I remember most of what you said."

"Okay." Nikki got up from the chair and dug in her jeans pocket and pulled out a candy bar. She laid it on the table. "You might need that, too." She strutted from the room.

Donavan rubbed his palms together and looked around the dining room. It was time to begin. He'd already changed his clothes and made a snack. For half an hour he'd watched his favorite action cartoon. When it was over, he'd turned off the TV and come into the dining room.

The dining room was a perfect place to study. It was quiet and he could concentrate without being bothered by anybody. Donavan pulled the DO NOT DISTURB sign he'd made earlier from his backpack and taped it to the door before he closed it.

DONAVAN BEGINS

STEP ONE

Donavan reviewed everything from the day's class: the drill, the class work, and the quiz.

STEP TWO

Setting the timer for fifteen minutes, Donavan selected five problems and began working on them.

STEP THREE

"These are not problems. They are equations that have to be solved," Donavan said calmly, and worked steadily until the small apple-shaped timer beeped. Immediately he reset the timer for five minutes.

STEP FOUR

"Thanks, Nikki," Donavan said, picking up the candy bar and taking a big bite. He got up from the table and decided not to begin a new project during the break; that would be a distraction. Instead, he went into the kitchen and poured a glass of juice to drink with his snack. He heard the timer beeping and ran into the dining room.

"Time to get back to work," he said cheerfully.

STEP FIVE

"This time I'm going to work for twenty minutes." Resetting the timer, Donavan worked on his homework until he completed every equation. "Finished!" he announced, and reached for the timer again.

STEP SIX

Donavan twisted the dial and set the timer for five minutes. He leaned back in the chair, smiled, and thought, *I'm on track.* He thought about all the plans he'd made, and remembered what his father had said: "It's hard to find a plan that fits. You've got to keep trying until you do." He hoped that his uncle would find a plan to walk again.

The timer beeped; his break was over.

STEP SEVEN

"I don't need this now," Donavan said, and moved the plastic apple aside. He slowly and carefully checked his homework. He made sure each set of equations was copied correctly and that there were no sloppy erasures. The papers were neat and clean.

He closed his math notebook and slid it into his backpack.

FRIDAY MORNING

"Hey Donnie! Donnie! Wait up!" He heard Eric calling him, but Donavan kept walking down the crowded hall. It was Friday afternoon, and he was on his way to math class. Donavan had worked the blended plan for two weeks. He had ten completed homework assignments. All he wanted to do now was finish this last class and start his weekend.

Heritage Month was two weeks away, and only six fifth graders had signed up to be greeters. *I'm in,* he thought gleefully.

"Hey, buddy," Eric said, tugging on Donavan's backpack. "What's your hurry? Didn't you hear me calling you?"

"Yes and no," Donavan said, turning to face Eric. "I want to get to class and make sure I'm ready for the quiz. What's up?"

"What's up is your mom, dad, and grandma going into the principal's office."

"What?" Donavan asked. "You sure?"

"Does Monday follow Sunday? Yes, I'm sure. I just

thought you'd want to know." Eric waited patiently for Donavan to react.

"I dunno," Donavan mumbled, shrugging his shoulders. "It's probably got something to do with Heritage Month." Donavan turned and walked toward the classroom.

"Oh," Eric said, disappointed. "I thought something had happened." He followed Donavan. "Hey, buddy, are you ready for the quiz?"

"Yeah, I'm ready. I've been doing great with my plan. I'm doing my math homework and understanding a lot more."

"Sounds good. I'm thinking about getting a strategy for science class," Eric said, walking toward a seat.

"See you after." Donavan waved and sat at his desk. *I wonder what they want,* he thought. Lots of parents and family were running in and out of the school. Heritage Month was just around the corner. He thought about Uncle Vic and dismissed the thought. Uncle Vic had said he wasn't ready to come to school. Mr. Sullivan clapped his hands. The class knew that it was time to begin.

Mr. Sullivan put the drill on the board and then asked the students to put their homework on top of their desks. While the class worked on the problems, Mr. Sullivan walked down the aisles checking homework.

If a student's paper had too many incorrect answers, he'd collect that page and go over it while the class worked on their assignments.

Donavan held his breath when Mr. Sullivan stopped at his desk.

"Ummm," Mr. Sullivan said, picking up the papers. "Mmm-hmm. Nice job." He laid the homework on the desk. Donavan noticed a green checkmark at the top on the paper. He exhaled slowly. Mr. Sullivan moved on.

After checking everyone's homework, Mr. Sullivan wrote five equations on the board. He announced that he needed five students to solve them. Donavan held his breath, crossed his fingers, and hoped that he would not be called on. He was unlucky.

"Donavan," Mr. Sullivan said. "Please go to the board and work out problem number three."

Donavan felt as if he had grown two extra fingers as he fumbled with his notebook. He dropped his textbook, paper, and pencil twice before he was able to gather his materials and head for the board. He felt as if fifteen pairs of eyes were drilling a hole in his back.

Softly Donavan repeated "optimistic, optimistic, optimistic" over and over until he felt calm. He stood in front of his equation and reviewed it carefully before he picked up a piece of chalk and began to solve it. After he finished, he looked around and noticed that the other students had sat down.

Donavan was at the board alone.

"Donavan," Mr. Sullivan said, "stay at the board and explain the steps you took to solve your problem." Suddenly Donavan felt hot. He wiped his clammy hands on his pants and looked at his classmates. They seemed untroubled by the heat. *It's a zillion degrees in here*, he thought, rubbing his neck.

In his mind, he heard Uncle Vic's words. "No distractions." Taking a deep breath, he tried to forget about the heat and the people looking at him. He remembered how carefully Nikki had explained that math problem to him. Using the chalk as a pointer, he took his time and went through each step. When he finished, Mr. Sullivan was smiling. The teacher walked over to the board and took a piece of chalk from the ledge.

"Good job, good job!" Mr. Sullivan said. "You did fine until you totaled your problem. He crossed off two zeroes and moved the decimal point two places to the left. "Do you see what you missed?"

Donavan looked at the problem and nodded. Mr. Sullivan gave Donavan a big thumbs-up.

"Keep up the good work." The compliment felt good. Donavan returned to his seat, smiling to himself. His first time at the board all week and he hadn't done all that badly!

Donavan began to copy the notes from the board and was almost finished when he heard his name over the classroom intercom.

"Donavan, you're wanted in the office," Mr. Sullivan said. "You'd better take your books. Class is almost over."

Donavan stuffed his books into his backpack and headed for the office. He wondered why he was being called there and suddenly a thought came to him. *Maybe Ms. Cassel is going to tell me I'm a greeter. Yes, that's it. I'm going to be a greeter!*

Donavan opened the office door, and instantly his good feelings drained away. His parents and grandma were standing in the office talking to Ms. Cassel, and their expressions were not happy.

Donavan's body temperature rose again, and he felt as if he had swallowed a swarm of bees.

"What's"—his voice squeaked—"up?"

No one answered.

"What happened?" He twisted his mouth to one side and scratched his neck.

His mother spoke. "Donavan Allen, a note, a letter, and several messages have been given to you to bring to school or take home." She looked at Ms. Cassel and continued. "Where are they? Not one has been received."

The disappointment he heard in her voice caused his stomach to churn like a blender. Again he felt like it was a zillion degrees.

"Donavan." His father's voice sounded like a drum. "I am very concerned about your actions." Before he could answer his father, Ms. Cassel spoke.

"Young man, I think we'd better have this conversation in my office."

Donavan glanced around, looking for a friendly face. His grandmother wasn't frowning, but she didn't look happy, either. Donavan remembered grandma's note and Mr. Sullivan's letter. The thoughts blew around in his mind like a hot wind, and the buzzing, churning bees in his stomach leaped to his head.

Just when things were looking up, he thought, and followed the adults into Ms. Cassel's office.

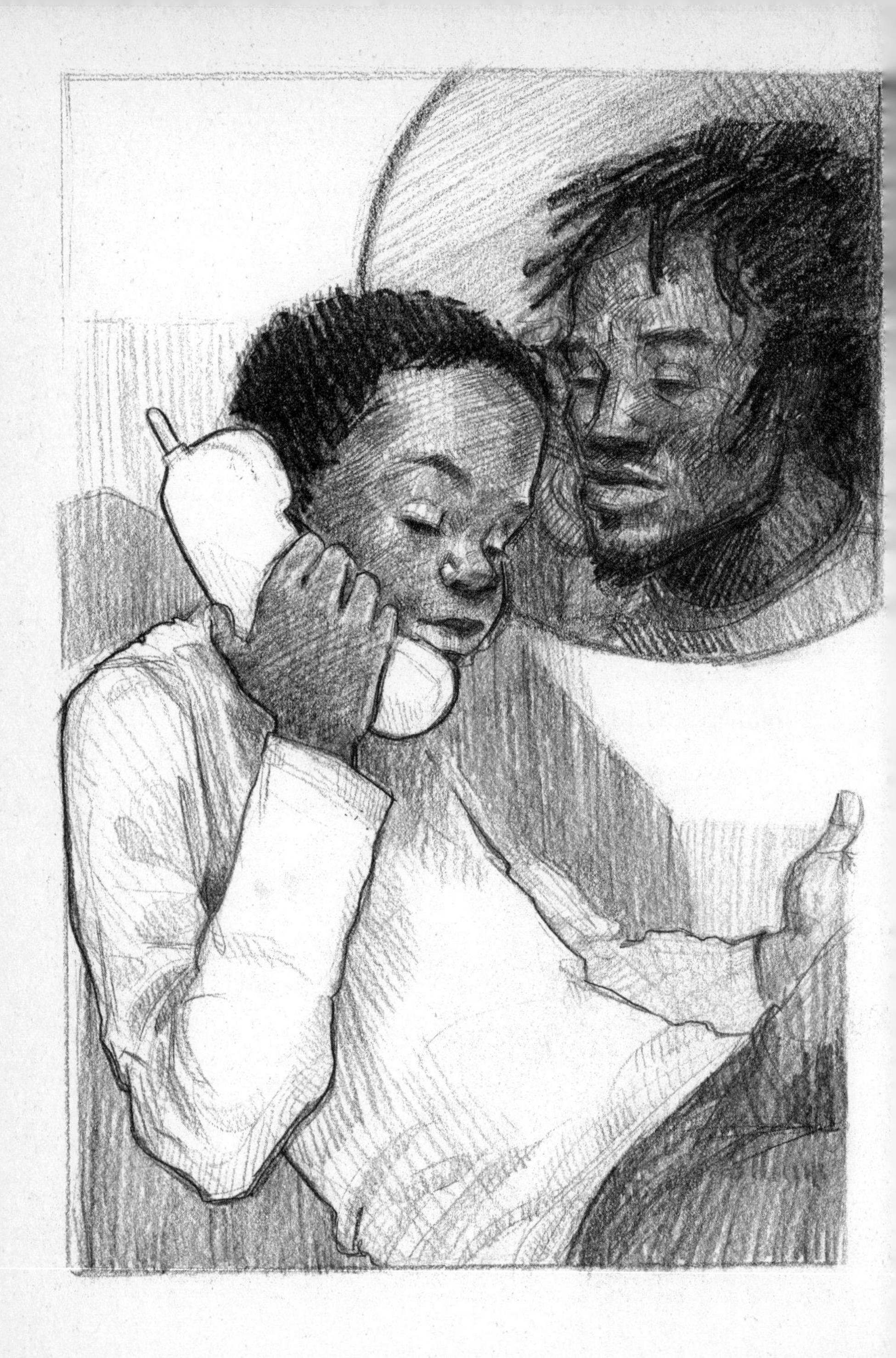

CHAPTER 14

HAVING A GOOD TALK

It was Sunday night and Donavan had one more thing to do before he went to bed. He punched the last four digits of Uncle Vic's number and waited for the phone to ring. He was nervous about what he had to tell Uncle Vic, but didn't have a choice.

Uncle Vic: Hello. Vic Carter speaking. May I help you?

Donavan: Hi, Uncle Vic. It's me, Donnie.

Uncle Vic: Hey, Champ. How you doing?

Donavan: Not so good.

Uncle Vic: How come? Is it the homework plan?

Donavan: No, no, the homework plan is great. I went to the board on Friday and got most of my equation right. I did only one thing wrong: I forgot to count off my decimal places.

Uncle Vic: Good, good. Just keep looking at your steps and saying them as you work on your equations.

Donavan: Umm. Ahh. I—I got to tell you something. (pause) Uncle Vic, do you remember the note Grandma talked about at your welcome-home dinner?

Uncle Vic: Kind of.

Donavan: Well, Grandma gave me a note to give Ms. Cassel. I kept the note and didn't give it to her.

Uncle Vic: Why not?

Donavan: I didn't think you wanted to come to school. (pause) At the dinner you didn't act like you wanted to come. And when I asked you that day in your house, the day you fell, you said you didn't want to come. Remember?

Uncle Vic: When you asked me that question, didn't you already have the note?

Donavan: Yes. I was just checking. I was checking to see if what I was doing was right.

Uncle Vic: Were you right, Champ? Did you do the right thing?

Donavan: No.

Uncle Vic: I *didn't* want to go to the school. But I had decided to go anyway. And that's why I was practicing walking with my legs. I explained that to you. Didn't I?

Donavan: Yes.

Uncle Vic: You were right in thinking about whether I wanted to come. But you were wrong in keeping that note.

Donavan: I know. I apologized to Dad and Mom and Grandma and Ms. Cassel. Plus, I kept a note Mr. Sullivan wrote to Dad and Mom. It was about my homework. I didn't want them to see it.

Uncle Vic: Champ, you been pretty busy breaking the law.

Donavan: I know.

Uncle Vic: You've been having a hard time, haven't you, Champ?

Donavan: Yep, but I was getting better in math. And . . .

Uncle Vic: And what else?

Donovan: I was getting . . . I was getting used to being around you, the way you are now.

Uncle Vic: Donnie, is there another reason why you didn't give the letter to Ms. Cassel? Were you uncomfortable with me coming to your school? (pause) Champ, I don't hold that against you. I wish I could have helped you, but I was having problems myself getting used to losing my legs. It's taking me some time.

Donavan: I didn't want the kids at school staring at you and asking you a lot of dumb questions. I didn't want them asking *me* questions.

Uncle Vic: Stares are something I'm getting used to, and questions . . . questions are people's way of trying to understand.

Donavan: You don't mind?

Uncle Vic: Sometimes I don't, sometimes I do. But I'm getting better at not minding.

Donavan: I'm getting better too. I still miss the way we used to hang out. But staying at your house—studying and watching TV and playing cards—I had a good time.

Uncle Vic: Good, 'cause I missed you. Being around you and your buddies was a big help. I hope to see more of you, and I'm going to follow your advice, Champ. I've got a plan. I'm going to open up a shop and restore furniture.

Donavan: Cool. And if it doesn't work, you'll try something else. Right?

Uncle Vic: Right.

Donavan: Uncle Vic, thanks for not being mad.

* * *

Uncle Vic: Thanks for owning up to what you did. And thanks for coming around to my house again.

Donavan: 'Bye.

Uncle Vic: See you later, Champ.

Donavan hung up the phone with a weary sigh. A lot had happened since Friday when he'd faced his parents, grandmother, and Ms. Cassel. They'd grounded him for a week, and he'd written a note of apology to Mr. Sullivan.

When his parents finally read Mr. Sullivan's note, they learned that he had asked them to come to school so that they could discuss finding a way to make things better for Donavan. Mr. Sullivan had written, "Donavan is a hardworking student. He is willing to improve. Can we find a way to help him?" After seeing that note, Donavan had felt terrible. What a dumb idea it had been to hide it. He'd thought he knew what was in the note and he had been so wrong.

"How you feeling?" The soft voice belonged to his grandmother. She had come to Sunday dinner. "I just wanted to say good night. Your father's taking me home."

Donavan raised his head, smiled, and sat up. "I just called Uncle Vic and told him about the note."

"Good for you." She sat on the bench next to him.

"I'm glad a new week is coming." Donavan sighed.

Grandma hugged him. "Things will be better. You learned a big lesson this week."

"I'm sorry I kept those letters, but Uncle Vic really didn't want to come to school."

"I know that," Grandma said, laughing.

"Then why did you want him to come?"

"Why did your dad want you to keep trying to find a way to overcome your math block?"

"He said you have to face difficult things. He said not facing what you fear only makes it worse." Donavan exhaled noisily. "And he sure was right."

"I know your uncle didn't want to visit the school, but I thought it might help him to get out and face people. Coming to the school would be a start."

"Grandma, I was wrong twice. I thought it was better if Uncle Vic didn't come and have the kids asking him dumb questions. I thought that if the kids stared at him it would be worse."

Grandma sighed. "Stares and dumb questions?" She thought for a moment before she said, "I guess he'll get some of that, but not everyone will do it."

"And I didn't give my parents Mr. Sullivan's note because I thought he had written something bad. I guessed wrong."

"Well," Grandma said, standing up. "You've learned

a valuable lesson. And you've handled it well." She smiled and patted him on the shoulder. "I'm proud of you."

"Thanks, Grandma. I feel kinda dumb." Donavan smiled shamefacedly.

Grandma laughed. "Donnie, maybe you were flummoxed for a while." She winked and left the room.

Donavan laughed. "Hey, Grandma, I already found that word. I used it for my math problem."

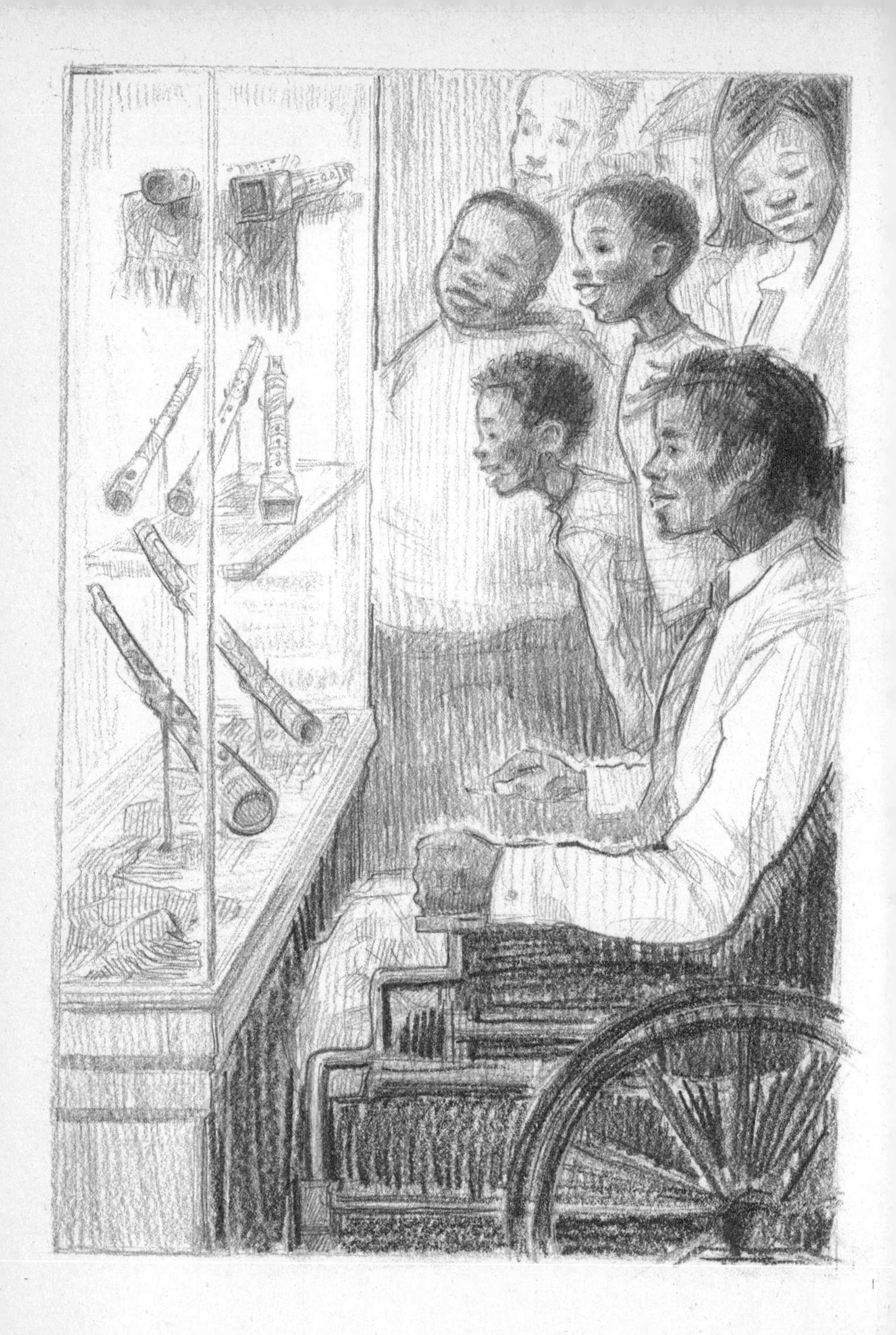

CHAPTER 15

HAVING A GOOD LOOK

My grandpop's movie was the best Heritage Month program we ever had!" Pooh boasted.

"Yeah, it was tight." Donavan kept writing. He was copying science notes from the board.

"Heritage Month is almost over and the kids are still talking about the movie."

"Pooh, lower your voice," Donavan warned, looking around the room.

"Yeah." Eric frowned. "Keep it down. Mr. Belts will make us move our seats if he thinks we're having a good time."

The boys looked around and saw Mr. Belts talking to a group of kids about a science project. Several students were busy setting up their lab kits.

Pooh opened his notebook and lowered his voice. "Pops was the tops!"

"Yeah, he was, so far. But you know there's still going to be the big program on the last night, next Friday." Eric set his science project on the desk.

Donavan pulled his science kit from the shelf over his desk and began unpacking it. "I can't believe Heritage Month is almost over."

"Do you guys know what Friday night's program is going to be?" Eric asked, looking at his two friends. "I've been asking around."

Pooh shook his head. "I've been snooping around the office, trying to overhear something."

"If we had been greeters, we would have found out," Donavan said.

"We tried, but the fifth graders were top choice," Eric said, shrugging his shoulders. "Anyway, we had great jobs. We were on the poster committee."

"It seems strange that we don't know anything about the last program and it's only a week away. I asked my grandma if she heard anything." Eric looked over at Donavan's kit to see if they had the same experiment.

"She tell you?" Pooh asked.

"Nope. She only talked about her batik workshop. The fourth graders made some nice bookmarks."

"Whatever it is, you know it must be B.I.G. This has

been the best Heritage Month we've ever had," Donavan said.

"I agree," Mr. Belts said. His voice surprised the boys. They had been so busy talking, they hadn't seen him coming to stand at their desks. "But I think every year is the best."

"I didn't fall asleep during any of the programs." Pooh sounded proud.

"Donavan," Mr. Belts said. "I knew your uncle Vic in high school. I played basketball with him."

"You did?" Donavan asked.

"If I give you a note after class, could you take it to him?" Mr. Belts asked.

Eric and Pooh nudged each other. Donavan ignored them. "I'll give it to him today," he promised.

"We'll go with him," Pooh and Eric added.

"Great," Mr. Belts said. "I saw them putting his carvings on display during lunchtime." The boys' eyes widened in surprise. Mr. Belts continued. "I play the flute, and when I saw his collection of wooden flutes I was impressed. Are they for sale?"

"I don't know," Donavan said, puzzled. "I knew that he carved wooden animals, but not flutes."

"Go and see them after class," Mr. Belts suggested. "Okay!" he said loudly. "Let's get started. We've got lots of work to do."

* * *

After science class Donavan, Eric, and Pooh hurried over to the school lobby.

"You didn't know about the flutes?" Pooh asked. "We sure didn't see any in your uncle's workshop."

"Nope, and I never heard anybody talking about flutes." Donavan searched his mind, trying to recall something. He couldn't.

In the lobby several teachers, a few parents, and many students were standing around the largest case. Miz Utz noticed the three boys. "Well, well, well, if it isn't triple trouble."

"Now we're a triple treat," Donavan said. He moved closer to the case and looked in. "Cool!" he said in awe, staring at the collection of wooden flutes of different sizes and shapes. Eric and Pooh moved to stand next to him.

"Man oh man!" Eric said softly, gazing at the flutes carved out of furniture legs. "Hey, Donnie," he whispered. "The legs. The legs in the basement."

Donavan suddenly remembered the pile of legs from old furniture that he'd seen in Uncle Vic's basement. "Holey moley! That's why he had those old things."

"Look at the carving on the tall flute," Pooh said.

Donavan was amazed as he listened to the comments of the teachers, parents, and students: "How beautiful!" "I love the shape of the green flute." "The wood is so smooth." "Did the artist really make flutes from the legs of furniture?" "How did he hollow the legs out?" "I wonder how they sound."

Donavan beamed, proud that they were talking about his uncle and what he had made.

"Excuse us. Folks, could you move aside for Mr. Johnson?" Donavan heard Ms. Cassel's voice and wondered what she meant. He turned from the case and saw his uncle sitting behind him.

"Uncle Vic?" he asked in surprise.

"Hello, Uncle Vic!" Pooh said. "You sure surprised us!" The crowd of people laughed.

Vic wheeled himself up to the display case. He didn't seem bothered by the stares or silence. "I wanted to come and see how my flutes were arranged. Yes, yes, yes." He nodded his head each time he saw a different flute. "They look great. I like the kente cloth they're lying on." He turned his head to look at Ms. Cassel.

Ms. Cassel grinned proudly. "I thought that was a good idea."

Miz Utz stepped out of the crowd. "Hello, Mr. Vic Carter," she said, reaching out to shake his hand. "I love your flutes."

"Thank you." Uncle Vic looked surprised and shy.

"It's wonderful how you've taken something old and discarded and created something new and beautiful."

Miz Utz stepped back to let Mr. Giles, the physical education instructor, shake Uncle Vic's hand. "Young man, I recognize the legs on that blue flute, the one on the bottom shelf," he said. "My grandma had a table with legs like that."

Anna Green, a third grader, asked, "Can you make music on those flutes?"

"Some you can," Uncle Vic said. "The longer ones are just for decoration."

Donavan stood back a little to watch the group. Uncle Vic was polite and friendly, answering as many questions as he could.

"People, people!" Ms. Cassel said loudly. "Mr. Johnson would be glad to answer your questions this Sunday when we have open house." Ms. Cassel looked around the lobby. "Sunday begins our last week. We will have open house for all of the parents, family, and friends who gave workshops and demonstrations. It will begin at three o'clock and end at six. Most of you will be there, so hold your questions until then." The adults in the group began to drift away. But the students crowded around the display, pointing and talking about the unusual flutes.

"Hello, fellows," Uncle Vic said. "I didn't know I'd see you guys."

"We're everywhere!" Eric said with delight.

"I didn't know you carved flutes," Donavan said. "They look so cool."

"I didn't tell anybody. I started carving in high school. In fact, I used to carve when I worked at the fire station and when I was in the National Guard. I started making flutes out of furniture legs because I hated to toss them away. I never thought they would be on display."

"Has Grandma and everybody seen them?"

"Not yet," Uncle Vic said sheepishly. "I called Alice, I mean Ms. Cassel, to talk about the animals, and I mentioned that I had some flutes, too. She thought they were more interesting."

"I wish I could have that one," Pooh said, pointing to a round flute. The end was carved in the shape of a fish.

"I'd like to have the skinny one with the owl carvings," Eric said.

"I'll bet my mom buys that one. She collects owls," Donavan said.

"Buy?" Pooh asked, raising his eyebrows. "I don't have enough money to pay for a flute."

"Maybe . . ." Eric looked at Uncle Vic and raised his voice. "We can find some work around a garage or a basement."

"Maybe," Uncle Vic said with a big wink.

CHAPTER 16

HALLELUIAH, HERITAGE MONTH

"There are so many people packed in here!" Donavan said.

"Why couldn't Breezy come?" Nikki asked her parents for the tenth time since they had left the house.

"What a crowd!" Grandma exclaimed, looking around the school gym.

"I see Pooh and his family," Mom said, waving her arms. "I think they're saving us some seats."

His father headed toward them. "We'd better hurry," he said.

The family moved along with the crowd. They called out greetings to their friends and neighbors. Excitement crackled in the air like electricity. Only Ms. Cassel and a few people knew what type of event the school was holding on the last day of Heritage Month.

"Hey, hey, hey!" Pooh yelled. Donavan and his family climbed the stairs and saw Aunt Weezie, Uncle Gilbert, and Vonda sitting in front of Pooh's family.

"Surprise! Surprise!" Vonda said, giggling. "Hey, Nikki, sit here."

"Glad you folks came. I was just thinking we couldn't save these seats much longer," Pop Grandville said, laughing. "Heritage Month has been great! I think I've been to every exhibit and workshop."

"Donnie!" Pooh sat next to Donavan, who scooted over. "Is Eric sitting with us?"

"I'm right behind you," Eric said, tapping Pooh on the shoulder.

Donavan watched Eric's grandmother sit beside Pop Grandville and Grandma. His parents were talking to Pooh's parents. Uncle Gilbert and Aunt Weezie were making sure Nikki and Vonda were comfortable. Looking around the gym, Donavan noticed one person was missing. He leaned over and touched his grandma's shoulder. "Grandma, where's Uncle Vic? I thought he was coming."

Grandma smiled and patted his hand lightly. "The evening is young."

Donavan was puzzled. "I invited him Sunday at the open house."

Grandma changed the subject. "I was surprised to see his flutes on display."

Pop Grandville looked at Grandma. "Everyone loves his flutes, Margaret. Think you can talk him into selling me one?"

"Vic said people ordered flutes at the open house. He'll have a lot of work." Grandma sounded happy.

"He's going to be busy," Eric's grandma added.

"I hope he keeps restoring furniture," Uncle Gilbert said.

"Pooh, Eric, and I are going to help Uncle Vic with his work," Donavan boasted. The three of them bumped their fists. Nikki and Vonda giggled and bumped their fists together too.

"Attention. May I have your attention, please?" Ms. Cassel's voice was loud and clear over the microphone She made motions with her hands for the crowd to stop chattering. Gradually people quieted and Ms. Cassel continued.

"This is the last night of Heritage Month. I know I say this every year, but this has been the best Heritage Month ever!" Ms. Cassel waited until the loud applause stopped before she continued. "We have a special program tonight." Murmurs blew around the room like a brisk wind until Ms. Cassel held up her hands.

"The group of men we are about to meet have come

to show us an old sport being played another way. This may be the first time for many of you. But it won't be the last." Ms. Cassel's smile was wide.

"I'd like you to meet the Blue Owl Warriors and the Flying Wheels!" The crowd was quiet, waiting. The large doors of the gym swung open, and two teams of men in wheelchairs rolled into the gym. The gym was silent until fast, snappy music with hip-hop rhythms started playing over the speakers. Everyone started clapping their hands to the music, and the teams began spinning their chairs around the floor to the beat.

One team wore electric blue jerseys with a large owl logo on the front. They rolled up the court, each spinning his chair with one hand and dribbling a basketball with the other.

"Families, meet the Blue Owl Warriors!" a voice boomed over the loudspeaker.

The other team rolled to the center of the court. They wore bright orange jerseys. Printed on the front of each were two large wheels with wings attached.

"Meet the fabulous Flying Wheels!" the referee hollered.

The Blue Owl Warriors tossed balls to each other in a zigzag pattern. They moved so fast it was hard to see which way the balls were going, but not one was dropped. The crowd clapped and cheered.

Nikki was jumping up and down, waving her hat in the air. "There's Uncle Vic, there's Uncle Vic!" she screamed.

"Number eleven!" Vonda yelped. "Uncle Vic is number eleven!"

Donavan recognized Uncle Vic, spinning a basketball on the tips of his fingers.

"Holey moley!" Donavan yelled, and plopped down on the seat. "That's one of Uncle Vic's old tricks." He watched Uncle Vic show off for the crowd. He spun the chair around in a circle and then leaned back until the front wheels lifted from the floor. "He's doing a wheelie!" Donavan yelled, and leaped to his feet. The noise level in the gym increased several decibels.

Ms. Cassel stepped back to the microphone. "Simmer down, folks, simmer down. Tonight we are going to have a game between the state's best wheelchair basketball teams. We're in for a treat." She clapped her hands.

The teams arranged their chairs in a double line formation. One by one the announcer introduced the men. When the announcer said, "I'd like to introduce the newest member of the Blue Owls, Vic Carter Johnson," Donavan, his family, and friends cheered the loudest. Uncle Gilbert and Pop Grandville whistled shrilly.

Miz Utz walked over to the microphone and began singing the National Anthem. The crowd joined in.

When the song ended, the referee tossed the ball in the air, and a man on the orange team slapped it down.

The game moved so swiftly the air in the gym seemed to crackle with energy and excitement. Donavan moved his head from side to side, trying to keep his eye on the ball.

Looking around, he noticed that some people were cheering. Others were urging the players on, and a few were even booing. The referee fouled an orange player, and there were several groans from the crowd. One man on the blue team was arguing with the referee.

"Don't let him score!" Donavan's father yelled.

"Stay on him! Stay with him!" Pop Grandville hollered.

The game was moving swiftly, each player wheeling with one hand and dribbling with the other. Donavan saw the fierce expressions they wore. Each man had come to win.

Then Number 11 was fouled. Uncle Vic positioned his chair at the free-throw line to make a long shot. Donavan held his breath and crossed his fingers until the ball cleared the net and toppled in. "Bam!" he shouted, and was on his feet again, cheering.

The orange team had possession of the ball. Number 20 was wheeling so fast that he collided with a blue player, Number 8.The chairs crashed and one overturned. Number 8 lay still on the floor, the wheels of his chair spinning.

"Ohhhh!" the crowd moaned, and then was silent. The teams crowded around the fallen player while the crowd held its breath. Seconds ticked by and then Number 8 sat up, righted his chair, and hopped on. The crowd went crazy; they stomped and cheered. The referee called the foul and the teams began to play ball again.

"My, my, my," Grandma said, shaking her head. "It's just too, too exciting."

"We won! We won!" Nikki shouted, shaking her paper pompons.

"Hip, hip, hooray!" Vonda screamed.

"What a game! What a game!" Pop Grandville sounded tired, but his smile was wide.

"I'm exhausted!" Grandma added.

The game was over and the Blue Owl Warriors had won by five points. Two of those points had come from Uncle Vic's free throw.

"If we're going to meet Vic, we'd better get outside," Dad said, moving down the steps.

Donavan watched his family and friends gather their coats and head for the exit. The players had left the floor five minutes earlier.

"You coming?" Grandma asked.

"I'm coming," Donavan answered. "I just want to sit for a minute." He looked at the empty basketball court.

"Hey, Champ, game's over." Donavan looked down and saw his uncle wheeling toward the bleachers. Uncle Vic's locks were pulled back into a ponytail. He had on a leather jacket and his ball was on his lap.

"I was just thinking," Donavan said, and stood. He walked down the steps toward his uncle. "Y'all played a great game. I could hardly keep up."

"You think?" Vic grinned proudly. "We need more practice."

"I thought the flutes were a surprise," Donavan said, standing beside his uncle. "But tonight blew me away. When did you decide to come?"

"Two weeks ago, when I visited the school to show Ms. Cassel the flutes, she was upset. She said that the speaker that she had for the last night couldn't come. I didn't think about the basketball team until I went to practice that night. I asked the guys if they had a free night. I told them about Heritage Month and they loved the idea."

"Doggone!" Donavan said. "We were lucky."

"Our coach said he would do it if I'd play with them." Uncle Vic shook his head. "Let me tell you, I was shaky. A lot of people here tonight knew me when I played ball in high school and college."

"You were brave," Donavan said, pleased.

"Well, it took me a while to get brave." Uncle Vic

chuckled. "What knees I have left were knocking."

Donavan laughed. "That's funny."

"Yeah, right."

"Then what happened?" He was still giggling at his uncle's joke.

"Then I called Alice, I mean Ms. Cassel, and told her my idea. I explained to her that most people have never and will never see a wheelchair basketball game. She said she thought they might like it."

"This game was a good surprise. Everyone was so excited. It was just like you said."

Uncle Vic looked puzzled. "Just like I said?" He raised an eyebrow.

"You said, 'It looks different. Instead of players running around, they are wheeling around.'" Donavan shook his head in wonder. "It is different, but it's really cool. Those guys are fast."

"You think so?" Uncle Vic asked, and wheeled his chair backward and then spun around. He tossed Donavan the ball. Donavan was so surprised he almost dropped it.

"Let's see what you got, Champ." Uncle Vic wheeled his chair downcourt toward the hoop. Donavan ran after him, dribbling. Uncle Vic slapped the ball from his hand.

"Huh?" Donavan ran around the chair, trying to

get the ball. His uncle wheeled backward and took a shot. The ball rose in the air, spinning, and then dropped neatly through the net.

"Kabam!" Uncle Vic said. "You're rusty, Champ." He wheeled his chair to recover the ball.

"Doggone!" Donavan said in awe. "Looks like I need a coach."

"Yeah. You need two coaches, one for math and one for b-ball."

Donavan laughed. It felt good to be playing ball and joking with Uncle Vic again. Vic threw him the ball and Donavan dribbled over to the free-throw line. He raised the ball and bent his knees and made the shot.

"Bam-bam!" he said. Uncle Vic clapped his hands in appreciation.

"I think you still got some juice. We need to work on that shot."

"Hey! What's taking y'all so long?" Nikki hollered from the gym door. "It's cold out here. C'mon."

Donavan and Uncle Vic looked at each and laughed. "It's time to go," Uncle Vic said. "I'm hungry."

Donavan held the ball and walked beside Vic's chair. "Hey, Uncle Vic," he said. "We make the perfect nephew-and-uncle team." He ran backward and tossed Vic the ball.

Uncle Vic caught it. "It's still true," he said in a husky voice.